The Lawmen

In 1885 a large band of half-breed Canadian rebels known as Metis, slip south over the border into Montana Territory. They carry with them a stolen Gatling gun and a strong desire to benefit, by any means, from the USA's wealth. Tough and experienced Deputy United States Marshal Jesse Bronson, is sent out to apprehend them. He is accompanied by a corporal of the Canadian Northwest Mounted Police. Bronson at first deeply resents the enforced presence of the red-coated Mountie and it is only after surviving numerous violent encounters that they finally begin to form a genuine bond.

The fast moving tale encompasses a bloody confrontation in the gold mining camp of Alder Gulch, followed by a pursuit down the swollen Missouri River on log rafts and then onto a final momentous showdown in the town of Great Falls.

The Lawmen

Paul Bedford

A Black Horse Western

ROBERT HALE · LONDON

ISBN 978-0-7198-1531-7

Robert Hale Limited
Clerkenwell House
Clerkenwell Green
London EC1R 0HT

www.halebooks.com

Typeset by
Derek Doyle & Associates, Shaw Heath
Printed and bound in Great Britain by
CPI Antony Rowe, Chippenham and Eastbourne

CHAPTER ONE

Considering that it was such a foul night, there were a surprisingly large number of tracks in the snow around Fallowfield's Trading Post. Perhaps its sheer frozen isolation was a possible reason. That and the fact that it was a well-known sanctuary to madmen and felons alike.

Jesse Bronson was certainly not the latter but, when considering what his intentions were, he could well have qualified as one of the former. As he scrutinized the structure before him, he choked down a cough that had been threatening to form in the base of his throat. Even a bearskin coat and thick woollen scarf could not completely ward off the biting cold. A film of frost had formed on his luxurious drooping moustache and there was a dangerous lack of feeling in his toes. He should really have removed the *single* glove that he wore, but he knew that there was then a serious possibility of his skin freezing to the metalwork on his 'sawn-off'.

One thing that he did do was to extract a badge from his pocket and pin it to the front of his hairy outer layer. Its shape resembled that of a medieval shield with a five-pointed star at its centre. There were four words etched on it, which completely justified his furtive presence at

Fallowfield's: Deputy United States Marshal.

The trading post consisted of a simple rectangular build-ing with stables tagged on and a worn hitching post out front. The gruelling conditions ensured that all the horses were under cover. Having tethered his mount to the extreme left end of the post, and so out of direct line of sight with the main entrance, Bronson then carefully approached the stables. A quick count told him that it contained eleven animals. Backing off, he then moved around to the rear of the main building. The hard-crusted snow crunched under-foot. In the gloom a solid narrow door beckoned.

Placing the sawn-off in the crook of his left arm, he lifted the catch and gently pushed. There was unexpected resis-tance. Cursing, he then placed his shoulder against the timber and heaved. It was all to no avail. The door was strongly bolted against all intruders.

'God damn you, Fallowfield,' he muttered. Did the fool really expect there to be petty pilferers on the prowl in such a desolate wilderness? Angrily moving on around the struc-ture, the lawman then reluctantly approached the more imposing bulk of the main entrance. His heart began to beat faster. Even though he had made it his trade, the dread of bloody violence never entirely left him. As a prelude to his admission, he released the buttons on his hulking great coat and then retracted both hammers on the shotgun.

The interior layout was known to him, the occupants of the post less so. He knew the men that he wanted, but not how many others might side with them. In such circum-stances he really should have had back-up, but recent events had not panned out in his favour. Sucking in a deep draught of perished air, Marshal Bronson tested the latch.

The door swung open easily and a fetid cocktail of sweat,

flatulence and tobacco smoke suddenly assailed him. Various grizzled individuals turned to appraise the new arrival, but before they could react, Bronson had pulled the door shut behind him and slipped off to his left. With his back pressed up against solid rough-cut timber, he gripped the shotgun and calmly surveyed his surroundings. An unnatural silence fell, as the room's occupants contemplated the possible reason for his very unwelcome presence. Only two or three actually recognized him, but the piece of tin on his chest more than made up for the shortfall.

The burly, shit-faced owner of the post asked the question on everyone's lips. 'Evening Marshal. What brings you to these parts?'

Fallowfield might just as well have been back in his home-town of Charleston, for all the notice that the other man took of him. Bronson continued his silent search of the large room until he spotted the two men that he wanted. They were sat in a poorly-lit alcove, well away from the bar. Keeping his back to the wall, the lawman edged over towards them. Only then did he state his purpose.

'I've got federal arrest warrants for Taylor Pruitt and Nelson Pruitt. All the rest of you can carry on about your business. I have no interest in you today.'

The two men that he *did* have an interest in glared at him with undisguised hatred. They both had the appearance of vicious gun thugs and seemed to be in an itching hurry to draw their weapons. What stopped them was the sight of the deadly sawn-off pointed directly at their table. Taylor, the elder of the two brothers, made a reluctant attempt at appeasement.

'You've got no call coming after us, Bronson. Robbing trains ain't a federal offence.'

The marshal sighed, before favouring them with an icy smile. 'Maybe not, but stealing the mail that they carry is. So think on this. If I have to trigger this big gun in here, we'll all likely lose our eardrums, but that'll be the least of your worries.'

His words carried a deadly intent that left no room for misinterpretation. The two outlaws silently locked stares with each other for a moment or two and then, as though intuitively reaching a decision, the tension left them. Taylor slowly placed his hands palm down on the table and his brother followed suite.

Bronson nodded in satisfaction. 'Very sensible, boys. Now stand up in plain sight and ease off those gun-belts.'

The two men had just got to their feet when suddenly everything went west. Off to their left a cadaverous individual with the look of a lunger rasped out menacingly, 'Listen good, law dog. You ain't taking *anyone* out of this piss pit!'

Hard experience had taught Bronson that such a challenge had to be met head on, otherwise he would completely lose control of the situation. So, without a word of warning, he swivelled to his right and fired the shotgun. In such a confined space the single detonation was ferocious. A huge cloud of black powder smoke erupted from the muzzle, completely obscuring his victim. Yet even the ringing in Bronson's ears could not blot out the dreadful screams.

Even as he returned his attention to the Pruitts, the marshal instinctively upturned a table and dropped to his knees. The two outlaws had leapt to their feet on either side of their own table and were now clutching revolvers. They both snapped off rapid shots at Bronson's makeshift barricade. Splinters flew from the solid top and a man nearby yelped in pain. 'God damn it to hell, Taylor,' he bawled. 'I ain't done nothing to you.'

The lawman came to a rapid decision and aimed his remaining barrel at the marginally more dangerous older brother. The contents of the twelve-gauge cartridge took that man squarely in the chest, throwing him back against the rear wall. The remaining Pruitt glanced over at his stricken relative in disbelief. The broken body was drenched with blood and twitching uncontrollably. Incandescent rage swept over him and he recklessly emptied his revolver into Bronson's tabletop.

As his weapon began to dry fire, one of the building's other hostile inhabitants bellowed out, 'Get the hell out of here, Nelson, or you'll be dead meat like your brother.'

With that the burly fellow took a run at the kneeling lawman. His intention was to kick Bronson in the head, but it didn't work out that way. Recognizing the new threat, the marshal hurled the empty shotgun at the approaching man and leapt to his feet. His assailant had to fend off the big gun and in doing so left himself open. The heavy iron hook, which had long before replaced Bronson's left hand, smashed into the man's jaw with sickening force. There was a loud crack and he crumpled to the floor with a howl of pain.

Flinging aside his heavy coat, Bronson drew his Remington Model 1875 revolver. He was aware that there was suddenly a lot of smoke in the room. The first man to die had unwittingly sent an oil lamp crashing to the floor. Fallowfield was now frantically beating out the flames with an old buffalo robe. With watering eyes, the lawman desperately searched about him. The man that he sought was no longer in the room. Cursing, he ran for the rear door.

'I'll kill any man that so much as looks crossways at me when I come back,' he yelled. With that, he slammed back the bolts with his hook and burst out into the frozen night. Nelson would either be lying in wait near the front door or riding for his life.

The thudding of hoofs on hard ground confirmed that the remaining train robber had chosen survival over valour. As the fugitive from rough justice pounded hell for leather into the trackless wastes, he bellowed down his back trail, 'You'll pay for this night's work, Bronson!'

With great regret but a deal of common sense, that man decided against pursuit. His horse was already well used and required food and rest, whereas Pruitt had had the choice of two fresh mounts. His arrest or demise would just have to be postponed until another day.

With the sweat already freezing on his forehead, the lawman padded cautiously towards the main door. He felt a strange urge to scratch his missing left hand. It was always the case in moments of stress. His Remington was cocked and ready. Any further opposition would be brutally answered.

On re-entering the trading post it was immediately obvious that there would be no more violence that night. The interior was in chaos and the remaining patrons were noticeably subdued. Two bloody corpses lay untended and the hardcase with an apparently broken jaw was desperately seeking relief in a whiskey bottle. Tables were overturned and damaged and oily smoke still rose from the timber floor. Bronson possessed a dark sense of humour and Fallowfield's obvious distress brought a wry smile to his face.

'Thanks for all your help, innkeeper,' he remarked sarcastically.

'Why the hell should I help you, Jesse Bronson?' that man responded sourly. 'Every time you come here, you kill my customers and wreck my place.'

The marshal was unmoved. He pointed at his first assailant whose upper torso was now a bloody pulp and remarked, 'That sack of shit called it a piss pit.'

As he moved off to inspect Taylor Pruitt's blood-soaked body, Fallowfield's instant comeback followed him, 'You don't have to like a place to spend greenbacks in it!'

Pruitt was dead as a wagon tyre, but thankfully his features were relatively unmarked. A positive identification would ease the payment of remuneration. Bending over the cadaver, Bronson proficiently emptied the pockets of anything valuable and then ordered a couple of men to heave it outside. Seeing their sullen reaction, he remarked, 'I killed him. I'm not going to carry him as well! If he stays in here, he'll start to turn and then we'll all suffer. Same goes for the other fellow.'

With that, he headed to the bar for an overdue shot of joy juice. As he tipped the bottle, Fallowfield regarded him with as much warmth as he was ever likely to display to anyone. 'You'd better watch yourself,' he offered. 'Kin can get wrathy about a killing. Nelson will, like as not, look to back shoot you after this night's work.'

Bronson regarded him calmly over his whiskey. His worn features displayed a lifetime's hard experience. 'And ain't that just always the way?'

CHAPTER TWO

'Just once it would be good if you brought a prisoner back alive, Jesse!'

'He called it, Bob. And besides, it saves you renting jail space off of the town. They're robbing bastards and all that paperwork will put you in an early grave.'

The two men were sat around a huge iron stove in the office of United States Marshal Robert Kelley. Winter had come early and hard in that year of 1885 and it was the first time either of them had been properly warm in many days. The marshal had the dubious privilege of dispensing federal law in the vast expanse of Montana Territory. To assist him in that thankless task he had a large number of deputies, of which Bronson was the longest serving. As they sipped gingerly from mugs of steaming coffee, the two lawmen maintained friendly eye contact. Although Kelley was undoubtedly the boss, they knew each other too well to maintain any noticeable formality.

'You shouldn't have gone out there alone, Jesse. The nation lost four good men last year and the tally's not over for this one yet.'

Bronson's features darkened at such talk. His own

partner had been fatally gut shot by an unexpectedly vicious counterfeiter only two months earlier. His death had been long and painful and he had left a widow and two young sons. 'Septimus was the only person I cared to ride with and he's gone. Anyhow, I work better alone. You know that.'

Kelley grunted and restlessly swilled his coffee around. He was fifty-four years old, with a heavy beard and full moustache. Basically decent and unusually honest, he valued the lives of the men that served under him and did not enjoy placing them in harm's way. From his demeanour it was obvious that he had something more on his mind than just the welcome demise of Taylor Pruitt.

'Well that situation's about to change,' he finally announced. Before the other man could contest that statement, he asked, 'Have you heard of Louis Riel?'

'Sounds like some kind of dance,' came the deliberately flippant response.

'Oh, he led them that all right,' replied Kelley in deadly earnest. 'Riel's some kind of big folk hero to a people called the Metis. They tried real hard to bring down the Canadian Government. His rebellion ended with a deal of violence back in May. Nothing to do with the US of A of course, except that some of his followers, led by Riel's right hand man, hightailed it out of Saskatchewan and over the border. That makes them my problem.'

Bronson regarded his boss curiously. There had to be more than just that troubling him. 'What's that to us? So long as they don't break any federal laws in Montana, they don't concern the marshals.'

Kelley favoured his subordinate with a look that spoke volumes. 'The US Attorney General, no less, has made it my problem. It appears that the Canadians are powerful keen to have their rebels back, especially the leader, a guy answering to the name of Jacques Labeau. Seems these sons of bitches also stirred the Cree Indians up real bad and nobody welcomes Indian trouble. The authorities up there want to put them on trial as an example to any other malcontents.' Then he added drily. 'It's just a shame it took them so long to ask. They don't seem to realize that we have winters down here as well.'

'How do we know that these *hombres* are still in the territory?'

Kelley was quick to scotch his subordinate's wishful thinking. 'The word is that they hope to bide their time here until the fuss dies down and then maybe trickle back across the border, but neither government is prepared to wait on "maybes".'

Bronson was beginning to get the drift and he didn't like the look of it one bit. 'So you expect me to round up these fellows all on my lonesome?'

'No. No I don't,' responded Kelley. His hairy visage was suddenly sporting a disconcertingly bright smile, which in itself was enough to make his deputy suspicious. Abruptly getting to his feet, the marshal carefully placed his tin cup on the stove and then strode over to a closed door. He opened it, poked his head into the next room and said, 'Corporal Bairstow, would you join us please?'

As heavy footsteps sounded, Bronson's mind performed cartwheels. 'Corporal! What the hell are the army doing getting involved in this? Are they treating it as an invasion?'

The large, heavily-bearded individual who entered the room only succeeded in posing more questions. He was clad in a bright red jacket, complete with roll collar and large pockets. Two chevrons decorated each sleeve. Below this came steel grey coloured cord breeches. Around his waist was a leather gun-belt supporting a flap holster of the type favoured by the cavalry. Bronson's first thought was that the 'God damned British Empire' had returned and in fact he wasn't far off the truth.

Kelley made the introductions. 'Jesse Bronson, meet Corporal Samuel Bairstow of the North West Mounted Police. He's what passes for a peace officer up in Canada. No offence intended.'

'None taken, sir,' boomed the really rather impressive Mountie. He moved towards the still seated Bronson and proffered his hand. That man made not the slightest attempt to take it. He'd just realized who his new partner was and he didn't take to the notion at all.

'This won't stand,' barked the deputy angrily. 'I can't go after renegades and gun thugs with someone I don't even know. For Christ's sake Bob, you know what it's like out there!'

Bairstow stood with his hand still outstretched and bristled with irritation at the perceived slight. 'It's the same for me,' he remarked heatedly. 'I'm down here under orders from my superintendent and I don't like it one little bit.'

'Superintendent,' responded Bronson incredulously. 'I thought they checked train tickets.'

'Enough of this,' snapped Kelley heatedly. 'You'll go along with this, Jesse, or you'll answer to me!' Before his subordinate could react, he abruptly held his hand up to indicate that he hadn't finished. 'There's something else. When these rebels dropped down over the border, they brought a Gatling gun with them. We have no idea what they intend doing with it, but however you look at it it's not good. Which is another reason why they are definitely our problem.'

Bronson's jaw moved, but no words came. A Gatling gun! With multiple rotating barrels turned by a hand crank, it could easily spew out over one hundred bullets per minute. Such a weapon in the wrong hands would be an absolute nightmare.

Still ignoring the proffered paw, he looked over at his superior and asked, 'Why did those sons of bitches have to pick Montana? What the hell was wrong with Dakota?'

The two mismatched lawmen maintained an uneasy silence as they spilled out of the building on to the street. Avoiding eye contact, Bronson chose instead to observe his surroundings in the weak autumn sunlight. He never ceased to be amazed at the speed with which the city of Billings was growing. With every visit, he noticed new structures. The metropolis had come into existence as a rail hub for the Northern Pacific Railroad and had spread outwards from either side of the tracks. The two men were standing in the commercial district to the north, where already most of the buildings were being constructed of brick. Civilization, with all its dubious benefits, was undoubtedly on the way.

It was the Mountie who finally attempted to break the impasse. Back out in the biting cold, he had pulled on a short buffalo coat, which to Bronson's mind at least had the benefit of hiding his garish jacket. Gesturing vaguely down the muddy street, Bairstow brusquely remarked, 'We're not going to get this job done by standing around sulking. We've both got our instructions and I suggest we leave at first light, so I'm for the livery to check on my gear. Then I'd be obliged if you'd point me out a good eating house.'

The American fumed at the other man's apparent assumption of leadership. No God damned Canadian was going to sashay down into his territory and start throwing his weight about. But instead of telling him straight, Jesse Bronson just had to go on the prod. It was his way and had got him into trouble on numerous occasions. As the two big men strode over to the livery stables, the needling began.

'So what's it like working for a woman then, Bearskin?'

The Mountie glanced over at him in obvious annoyance. 'The name's *Bairstow* and I wouldn't know. I've never met with Queen Victoria.'

'Yeah, yeah, but you're part of her thin red line aren't you, Bearskin? Part of the bloody British Empire.'

The Mountie kept on walking, but his back had somehow got straighter and more rigid. He appeared to be mulling over a response and finally it came. 'You can think what you like about the British or Canadians or any other damned race, but I'm just down here to do a job, so back off. *And* the name's still *Bairstow!*'

As they approached the entrance to the livery, the so-called 'peace officer' just couldn't help himself. 'So how come these rebels managed to get hold of a Gatling gun? You mounted police didn't just happen to misplace one did you? Hey, did you, *Bearskin?*'

The blow was so powerful and so unexpected that it shook Bronson to his core. A wave of nausea swept over him as he crashed back against the heavy stable door. Tears streamed down his battered face as he tried to account for the sudden shocking pain. Then, before he could make sense of it all, his gut seemed to explode under the force of a clenched fist. With an awful groan, he doubled over and collapsed on to the earthen floor. Although his whole body seemed to be wracked with pain, it was the distinctive taste of blood in his mouth that saved him. The awareness that

17

the poxy 'John Bull' had made him bleed provided sufficient stimulus to bring him to his senses. One way or another there would have to be a reckoning.

Bairstow had stepped back to recover his balance prior to launching a kick at the marshal's unprotected stomach. It was then that he suddenly observed for the first time the curved hook protruding from his opponent's left sleeve. Recognition of its lethal potential brought on a moment's hesitation.

Taking advantage of the fleeting respite, Bronson forced himself into action. Swivelling on the ground, he stretched out his right leg and swept it round in an arc. His booted foot hooked round behind the back of Bairstow's left leg with enough force to topple him. Unable to stop himself, the Canadian fell heavily to the ground. Winded, he was temporarily helpless but, luckily for him, his opponent was unable to take advantage of the fact.

Bloodied and sore, Bronson scrambled to his feet. By the time he had wiped the tears from his eyes and got his bearings, the Mountie had sucked some chill air into his lungs and also hauled himself upright. But that man wasn't quite fast enough to anticipate his adversary's retaliation.

With raw anger coursing through his veins, the marshal charged across the intervening space and smashed into the other man's torso. The momentum was enough to take them both into an empty stall and down on to the ground. This time though, Bronson had the advantage because he was on top. Yet sadly for him, his vicious head butt was only partially successful. Bairstow had turned away just enough to avoid having his nose broken, but still received a stunning jolt. Getting astride his opponent, Bronson clenched his right fist. Even though he was thirsting for revenge, something inside made him hold back from using his left arm as a potentially lethal club. Such unaccustomed restraint didn't prevent him from landing two telling blows. His bruised knuckles came away greasy with blood. Then, on the point of landing a third, he suddenly reeled sideways as Bairstow's right knee slammed up into his lower back. Even as he fell into the side of the stall, it occurred to him that his opponent had to be as strong as a tree to be able to come back from such violent treatment.

The stout timber held firm against his weight and Bronson reached out to pull himself to his feet. As he did so his right hand closed over a leather bridle. Yanking it from the top of the partition, he lashed out at his opponent. The rawhide caught Bairstow a stinging blow on his temple.

'You whore's son,' that man bellowed out. 'I'll settle you for that.' So saying, he pulled a wicked looking skinning knife from his left boot and lunged forward. Bronson only just managed to twist aside, but even so he felt a stinging pain along his ribs. The realization suddenly hit him that Bairstow was quite prepared to use deadly force to resolve the matter. Dropping the bridle, he grabbed the Mountie's wrist and endeavoured to force the blade from his grip. Even as he did so, he felt clawed fingers reaching for his eyes. All inhibitions left him and he raised his left arm to deliver a crushing blow.

The tremendous detonation in the building was sufficient to cause both men to freeze. As a cloud of acrid smoke wafted towards them, an aggrieved voice cried out, 'Leave it be, you God damned saddle tramps. There'll be no brawling in my place.'

Slowly and reluctantly the two men disentangled themselves. As they turned to face the livery's owner, a smoking shotgun held menacingly before him, a look of disbelief – quickly followed by bewilderment – spread over that man's grizzled features. Not only had he instantly recognized the lawman, he had also caught a glimpse of Bairstow's bright red jacket. Assuming that the United States must have somehow declared war on the British Empire again, he protested unhappily, 'Sweet Jesus, Marshal, can't you beat on your prisoners someplace else?'

CHAPTER THREE

It was a slightly chastened Jesse Bronson who urged his mount out into the Montana wilderness the next morning. His jaw ached and the superficial knife wound stung unpleasantly, but that was only the half of it. He had received a visit from an unusually vitriolic Marshal Kelley in the small hours. That man had learned of the unseemly fracas between his deputy and the visiting Canadian and for some strange reason had immediately assumed that Bronson was to blame. Being directly answerable to the attorney general for the condition of their visitor, Kelley had stated his displeasure in no uncertain terms. Apparently, numerous years of friendship and loyal service would count for nothing if there were any repetition. Bronson would be out in the cold, figuratively and literally. Every pimp and murderer that harboured a grudge against him would learn that he was no longer a federal officer. Strong words indeed, and they had actually been enough to rattle the hardened deputy.

The two riders headed on down towards the Yellowstone River. Because they had no real idea how long their mission would take, they were both leading heavily laden pack mules. Although such animals could slow them down, speed was not really an issue. With winter fast approaching it was survival that counted. Both men maintained a stubborn angry silence, which even the notoriously obstinate Bronson realized would have a crippling effect on their chances of success if it were to continue. He also reluctantly accepted that, after the previous day's boorish events, it would have to be up to him to initiate any conversation.

Reining in on the riverbank to allow the animals to drink, he twisted in his saddle and peered grumpily over at his companion. In addition to his buffalo coat the Mountie was wearing a fur hat and mittens, but there was no hiding the black eye and bruising to his face. Uttering a deep sigh, Bronson took the bull by the horns.

'If this rebellion occurred in May, how come it took six months for you to get down here?'

Bairstow favoured him with an appraising glance. It was obvious that he was searching for any sign of renewed provocation. Finally deciding that the question could be genuine, he responded with, 'I suppose it was simple pride! The folks in Ottawa didn't want to admit that their problems had spilled out across the border. I recall that your government wasn't too happy when Sitting Bull's Sioux fled up into Canada.'

Bronson grunted. 'Good answer,' he considered grudgingly. 'These rebels. Any idea what their intentions are down here?'

'You're asking me?'

The marshal sighed again. He supposed he probably deserved that. 'I know Montana, but I don't know your people. I expect that's why they put us together.'

The Mountie's battered face creased into a wary smile. 'They are a brutal and ruthless group of men. I suspect that they will want to steal as much from you wealthy Americans as possible, before they return to their own lands. They are used to the wilderness and will doubtless prefer to keep clear of large towns, so it's for you to decide where they might strike. Don't forget, they have been in Montana for some months, so they have had time to check out the land.'

As their animals slaked their thirst in the shallows, Bronson's mind was working overtime. All his illogical enmity towards Bairstow was temporarily forgotten. It didn't take him long to reach a decision. 'There are gold and silver mines well to the west of here. The richest diggings are at Alder Gulch. There'll be guards, but with their big gun, they could pretty much help themselves.'

'Sounds sensible enough to me. Everybody's heard of that place, although north of the border we know it as Alder Creek,' remarked the Mountie. 'I reckon we should head on over there for a look see. If you take point, I'll follow on behind. I expect that'll suit you just fine.'

Bronson glanced at him sharply. 'I suppose I had that coming, but don't push it. We don't want to get to fighting again out here.'

For the rest of that day the two lawmen travelled west across the northern Great Plains. With winter already with them in everything but name, the terrain possessed an air of desolation lightened only by the continued presence of the river on their south flank. The fast flowing water sparkled so cheerfully in the sunlight that one could temporarily forget the biting chill. They would follow the course of the Yellowstone for perhaps half of their journey, before it turned south in the foothills of the Rockies. Until then they would have an ample source of water and an opportunity to feed off the game that it attracted.

Bronson, as befitted a seasoned lawman, set a cautious pace. Periodically he carefully scrutinized the landscape, including their back trail, through a pair of powerful field glasses. He hadn't survived years in the wilderness by being headstrong. Corporal Bairstow, recognizing this fact, was content to follow on in his wake. In doing so, the Mountie took the time to observe the man that he had been part-nered with. He put Bronson at around forty years old, but could quite easily have been five years off either way. The most striking thing about him was his eyes. They were quite simply never still and their continuous movement seemed to be instinctive, rather than requiring a conscious effort. The marshal gave the impression of being simultaneously both the hunter and the hunted.

That night they camped in a shallow depression by the river-bank, with the intention of benefiting from its protection from the constant wind. The ground was so hard that they had to hammer in the metal picket pins that they used to secure the animals. Due to the night-time temperatures, a cold camp was out of the question. The risk from lighting a fire seemed slight, as Indian trouble was unlikely and the men that they were pursuing could not yet know of their presence. Bronson utilized one of the precious Lucifers that he kept in an old cartridge case sealed with wax, so ensuring their protection from moisture. Both men were used to living rough, so their equipment was very similar. Yet one item of bedding drew envious glances from the Mountie. With an unnecessarily theatrical flourish, Bronson produced a large rubber blanket, which he had purchased from back east by mail order.

'This'll do the job every time,' he remarked with undue satisfaction. 'Keeps the damp from creeping up into my old bones and stops the rain soaking my possibles.'

'Seems you live pretty high down here,' responded Bairstow with more than a touch of sarcasm. 'I couldn't count the number of snow drifts I've had to endure with just this old buffalo coat around me.'

Bronson's come back was swift and remarkably ill-considered. 'If we're into tall tales, then I could trump you whenever I choose!'

'I'm sure you could, Deputy,' replied Bairstow with a slow smile. 'Very likely you've had plenty of practice.'

The next day dawned crisp and bitterly cold. Bronson knew without doubt that once they got into the foothills of the Rockies, snow would be inevitable. The question was: would that affect the activities of the insurgents – if indeed that was where they were? As he coaxed the campfire back into life, he posed a serious question. 'Just how tough are these sons of bitches that we're after, anyhow?'

The Mountie was running on the spot to get his circulation going and seemed happy to take his mind off the chill. 'They could be a mixture of English-speaking half-breeds and a people known as the Metis. Those devils are French-speaking half-breeds who wanted to keep to the old ways at all costs. I imagine that it's more likely to be them that we are after. The Metis consider any form of authority to be their mortal enemy and as a policeman I represent the Canadian Government.'

'Oh great,' responded Bronson with feeling. 'So we're not just hunting a bunch of "road agents", they have to be real live fanatical revolutionaries.'

'Well from the look of all the weaponry you're carrying, you're loaded for bear, so they shouldn't trouble you any,' replied Bairstow. His practised eye had long before taken in the marshal's 45/70 Winchester in a leather scabbard and the twelve-gauge shotgun hanging by a strap from the saddle-horn. Then there was the solid framed Remington in his gun-belt, which always came in useful for pounding felons over the head. God knows what else he had upon his person.

'Walk carefully and carry a big stick. That's my motto and it's served me well so far.' There was no hint of bravado in Bronson's remark. He fully intended to live long enough to see Montana become a state with its own senators and representatives. Unlike some deputies, he didn't work purely for the money. He actually had pride in the territory that he served.

That day pretty accurately replicated the first. Bronson again took the lead. His field glasses revealed nothing of either concern or interest to them. At noon they watered the animals in the Yellowstone and chewed beef jerky in the saddle. After a short break they resumed their relentless trek westward. The terrain remained flat and featureless, but even on the prairie there are undulations sufficient to hide someone who wishes to.

The bullet flew past Bairstow's fur hat with a sound like a bee in flight. Even in the numbing cold, both men's reactions remained sharp. Cursing fluently, they seized their Winchesters, slid from their saddles and dropped down on to the hard ground. Another shot rang out. This time the projectile struck a rock some yards away and whined off into the frozen air. The noise was sufficient to spook the animals and they fled at speed.

'Damn, damn, damn,' intoned Bronson. It looked like someone would have a quantity of walking to do.

'Whoever's out there can't shoot worth a damn,' commented the Mountie, but nevertheless he kept his nose down to the frozen earth.

'Federal officers,' bellowed out Bronson. 'State your name and business here.' Without waiting for an answer, he placed the Winchester's forestock within the confines of his hook and levered in a cartridge. 'Don't you go popping any more caps,' he added. 'Or it'll go badly for you.'

An eerie silence was all that greeted the marshal's forthright challenge. Whoever had attacked them had to possess a horse, but there was no sign of one, unless it was hidden over by the riverbank. Yet that was half a mile away. Thankfully, his field glasses were still round his neck, so Bronson began a careful search of the terrain before them. As his glasses crept slowly over the harsh landscape, he heard Bairstow chamber in a cartridge. That man then crept forward, but sensibly maintained his distance. 'Anything?' he queried.

'Not a—' Then Bronson saw it. There was a horse all right, some two hundred yards away, but it was dead and being used as a fort. Grey in colour and low to the ground, it was not surprising that it had remained invisible to the naked eye. Unslinging the glasses, he handed them to his companion and pointed out his discovery. 'What kind of shot are you?' he demanded.

Bairstow gazed at him incredulously. 'Well I reckon maybe I just might be able to hit a dead horse at a couple of hundred yards!'

The American appeared unimpressed, but had already

made his plans. 'So you fire and I'll run. Then I'll do the same for you. Ready?'

The Mountie levelled his rifle and grunted acknowledgement.

'Fire!' hissed Bronson. Off to his right, the first shot rang out and he leapt to his feet and ran like hell, zigzagging from side to side. Sucking in cold air, he could feel his heart pounding, but he kept on going full chisel. Bullets were rapidly slamming into the dead animal and there was no return fire. Bronson had to admit that his companion knew his business.

'Out,' came the cry and the marshal dropped to the ground. His chest was heaving, but he was now less than one hundred yards away from their assailant. At that range he didn't need to allow much time for his breathing to settle. As soon as Bairstow had reloaded, Bronson squeezed off the first round. As he worked the lever action with practised speed, a cloud of sulphurous smoke built up before him, but it didn't affect the accuracy of his covering fire. After the first bullet had hit the cadaver, he continued to send a stream of lead on to the target. Bairstow pounded over the hard ground and then dropped down nearby. To anyone viewing the scene, it would have been quite obvious that two time served professionals were at work.

'There's something strange about all this,' remarked the Mountie thoughtfully. 'Either he's hit or he's saving everything for the first of us to get to him.'

'Well it had better not be you then,' replied the marshal resolutely. 'You're showing a mite too much colour and there'll be the devil to pay if you end up dead!'

The Canadian's coat had opened with the exertion and his bright red jacket indeed made him an excellent target.

Before the Mountie could protest, Bronson threw off his heavy coat and called out, 'Ready?'

At the first detonation, he was up and off. He bitterly regretted the fact that his shotgun was somewhere along his back trail. It was ideal for close quarter rushes. As he drew closer, the pounding in his chest was no longer due to exertion alone. His mouth was dry with raw fear and the sweat on his forehead was also not just the product of physical effort. Just what the hell was awaiting him behind that dead horse?

At the last moment, he leapt off to his left and came around the side of the fort in a wide circle. Bairstow was out of shells again, but it no longer mattered. Bronson's rifle, awkwardly supported by his hook, was suddenly superfluous. The burly individual lying next to his blood-spattered horse had been gut shot, but not by either of the lawmen. Judging by the mess coating his shabby waistcoat, he was a long time dying. Pain-wracked eyes slowly rose to meet the marshal's appraising stare. That officer's opening comment was not what the mortally wounded man might have expected to hear.

'We've wasted a whole mess of cartridges on you, mister. I don't welcome people taking shots at me, so before you take your last breath you've got some explaining to do!'

By way of response, a bloody froth foamed out over the man's whiskery face. He finally managed one word. 'Water!'

It was common for a dying man to be afflicted by an intense thirst and Bronson knew that if he were to gain any information he would have to satisfy it. His own canteen could have been anywhere by then, but conveniently their erstwhile assailant had a full one nearby. Gratefully slaking his own thirst first, he then bent down and held it to the lips of the desperate patient. As the cold liquid was greedily and noisily consumed, Bronson observed the Mountie cautiously approaching the fort. Indicating the seeping wound, he remarked, 'This mess is none of our doing, but if we're lucky this fellow's going to set us straight before he meets his maker.'

'You're all heart, Deputy,' observed Bairstow bleakly.

'You were nearly kilt by his first shot, so. . . .'

'Name's Thomas,' sputtered the man before them. His breath came in short rasps and it was obvious that the effort required to talk was costing him dear. His eyes were locked on to Bronson's chest. 'Didn't know you were badged up. Sent from Alder Gulch for help.'

Now that did get the marshal's full attention. All of a sudden Thomas's survival gained importance. 'Take it easy fella. We'll see about making you more comfortable.'

Summoning all his strength, Thomas grasped Bronson's hand. 'I'm a dead man and you know it, but I took at least one of the bastards with me. He's back there a ways.'

Bronson looked pointedly at the Mountie. That man nodded, levered up a round in his reloaded Winchester and took off.

'They were on my trail soon as I set off,' Thomas continued with desperate determination. 'Just couldn't shake 'em. Once they'd brought me down, they hightailed it. Guess it wasn't worth losing another man just to take my things. This old Spencer kept spitting lead at them.'

'Who were they?' interrupted Bronson urgently.

'Some kind of Frenchie half-breeds. Murderous devils to a man. Taken over the diggings.'

Thomas abruptly stopped talking. His breaths were coming shorter and faster. Every word had brought forth more blood. He was obviously near the end. Bronson made to rise up, but the other man maintained a manic grip on his hand. It was then that he falteringly uttered the last six words of his life.

'Don't . . . let me die . . . alone, *please*!'

Bronson possessed a resolutely cynical view of life, but Thomas's desperate plea unexpectedly found a chink in his armour. The two men remained connected, eyes locked, until death claimed its latest victim. Bairstow found them like that when he finally returned.

'I don't even know whether Thomas was his first or last name,' remarked the marshal dejectedly. There was a sadness about his eyes that the Mountie hadn't witnessed before and it made him feel strangely uncomfortable. Only two days earlier, he had been attempting to gut the American with a skinning knife and yet he now felt the beginnings of a totally unexpected warmth for him. It didn't last long however. As though shaking off a heavy coat, Bronson's sorrowful mood abruptly left him and was replaced by pure avarice. Without any sign of embarrassment, he swiftly patted down the body and removed anything of perceived value. Bairstow, whose father had been a preacher, had been raised to be scrupulously honest. On joining the recently formed North West Mounted Police, he had naturally continued that tradition and somewhat naively expected it of others. In an effort to hide his confusion, the big bluff Canadian blurted out his own news.

'It's one of the rebels all right. I'd recognize a Metis anywhere. So it looks like your hunch was correct.'

Bronson slowly drew away from the dead man and got to his feet. Their animals had bolted a fair way down their back trail and like most horsemen he didn't relish the thought of walking anywhere. He summed up his reaction to Bairstow's revelation with just one word. 'Wonderful!'

CHAPTER FOUR

Kirsty Landers had been in a state of constant dread for over a month. She had thought that it couldn't possibly get worse, but the previous day's events had proved her wrong. Her father, Kirk, had been shot down before her very eyes and now lay in the dispiriting hovel that was their temporary home, poised on the cusp between life and death. The bullet was lodged somewhere deep in his chest. Probing the wound had been traumatic and Kirsty had then decided that, unless they wanted to kill him, any extraction would have to be left to someone with medical training. Unfortunately the camp's only doctor had recently died of consumption. Her heightened anxiety was compounded by the fact that after examining Kirk's heavy coat, she knew beyond doubt that a small portion of the grubby material had been carried into the wound.

As if all of that wasn't enough, there was the additional factor of her own personal peril. The aftermath of the sudden act of brutal violence had brought her to the unwelcome attention of the marauders' leader. He went by the name of Jacques Labeau. Not that she really gave a damn what he was called. All she knew was that he was a foul-mouthed, debauched and violent half-breed who had brought fear to the mining community of Alder Gulch and now seemed keen to expend his sick lust on her.

'You need to get some provisions together, saddle a horse and clear off out of here as soon as darkness falls,' Deckard Foster earnestly advised. 'I mean it, Kirsty. Go while you can, before either Labeau or the weather gets you.'

The young woman regarded her father's oldest friend solemnly. He was a massive bear of a man with a huge mane of black hair. Normally he and his cronies would have swatted a vile insect like Labeau as soon as he had started throwing his weight about. Foster was charged with protecting the diggings from thieves, claim jumpers and any other miscreants that fetched up in Alder Gulch. No one had seriously challenged his authority until the Metis had turned up with a Gatling gun! What chance did men armed with trap-door Springfields and a few repeaters have against a weapon like that?

'I can't, I won't leave my pa like this.' Kirsty's voice contained a hint of hysteria, but there was no doubting her determination. She was a fine looking brunette in her mid-twenties with an enviable figure, who had managed to keep her head down until the incident with her father. 'You know damn well that it was Labeau who ordered the shooting. If that half-breed comes near me, I'll gut him like a fish.'

Foster knew that he was wasting his time, but he tried once more anyway. 'That's fighting talk and we can't protect you against those sons of bitches. We're outnumbered and outgunned. The only reason we're still alive is because he needs us to do the work. We've just got to hope that Thomas Cates gets back with some law and a sawbones. That's if he's

34

still alive!'

'Which is why I've got to stay here, Dec. Someone's got to look after my pa until he gets some proper doctoring. And you said yourself that Thomas knows how to handle that old Spencer of his.'

It was the next day when, after following an intermittent blood trail, they found the second body. There was a large hole in the man's chest and an even larger exit wound: testimony to the fact that Thomas had definitely known how to use President Lincoln's 'secret weapon'. The face might once have been handsome with its high cheekbones, but death had frozen its features in a position of contorted agony. A large pool of blood had congealed around the torso before it had had the chance to drain on to the bone hard ground. The body was stripped of all its belongings, including footwear.

'His *compadres* were all heart,' remarked Bronson dispassionately. 'They let him ride along with them until he died and then they cleaned him out.'

Bairstow regarded him with vague distaste. 'Before *you* got chance to, you mean?' He had witnessed the lawman go through Thomas's pockets the previous day and he had seen the disappointment on Bronson's face when he had looked over the body of the first assailant. Like the latest one, it too had had anything remotely valuable removed.

The marshal managed a very fair display of righteous indignation. 'Now see, there you go jumping to hasty conclusions. I only took his purse and mementos in case he has any relatives in Alder Gulch. It's my duty as a lawman.'

'Along with his watch and his kerchief and boots.'

'Exactly. It's little things like that his kin would treasure.

I'll tell you one thing,' Bronson added, suddenly anxious to get off the subject. 'Those Metis of yours went to a powerful amount of trouble to run our friend Thomas to ground. It takes a lot of fear or greed to push scum like this into risking their lives. Whoever's leading the pack must be quite some *hombre.*'

The Mountie favoured him with a keen glance. 'I reckon you're right on the nail there . . . and I believe I know him!'

Jacques Labeau slammed the point of his vicious looking skinning knife into the table before him. 'I want that girl real bad! She's the best thing I've seen in this flea-ridden camp.'

His companions regarded him dubiously. They all wanted that girl, but there were several large reasons why they hadn't taken her. Deckard Foster and some of the others had made it plain that the Metis would have to come through them first. With their vastly superior fire power this was quite possible, but then the marauders would have to do more of the physical work and that did not suit them at all. Her father had only taken a bullet because he had bravely, some might say foolishly, attempted to resist their demands for greater efforts in recovering the gold. That violence was easily justified because it was purely business.

Marcel cautiously placed his hand on Labeau's shoulder. He was the only man who could contemplate such a gesture, but even he had to be careful. He spoke slowly in a soft crooning voice. '*Oui, mon chéri.* She is all woman, is that one, but think on. When we have finished in this camp, you will have enough money to buy a hundred or even a thousand like her. *And* you won't have to kill to get them.'

Labeau tensed under his subordinate's hesitant contact.

He did not care to be touched by anybody unless it was during sexual congress. His dark, pitted features tightened as he fixed his penetrating gaze on the other man. Although of slim build and only medium height, the rebel leader seemed to exude an aura of permanent menace and few that knew him came too close. It was as though the perceived shame of his mixed parentage had imbued him with a sense of outrage and anger that he was always struggling to control. This had been exacerbated by the savage beatings that his father, a French fur trader, had meted out to him on the slightest pretext. But there was far more to Labeau than barely-suppressed violence. He possessed an almost animal cunning and was unusually intelligent for a simple frontiersman.

'I like to kill, Marcel,' he remarked softly, shrugging clear of the other's hand. 'But I suppose I can bide my time. There will be an occasion when those *cochons* that watch over her are distracted and then I will strike.'

Labeau suddenly relaxed and let his eyes sweep over the other men present in the large timbered cabin. Upon seizing control of Alder Gulch, the Metis had appropriated the best accommodation for themselves and they used this particular building as a meeting house. It was slightly elevated and situated at the head of the single rudimentary street that bisected the mining camp. Outside its solid door sat the squat intimidating shape of their Gatling gun, mounted upon a tripod. That fearsome weapon, transported south in pieces on pack mules, was permanently manned by shifts of never less than three men. It was illuminated throughout the night by the light from numerous burning torches coated with pitch.

Abruptly changing the subject, Labeau switched on to

another favourite topic. Addressing his lieutenants, he demanded, 'Now, tell me about the colour. How much flake do we possess? How pure is the ore?'

Another bitter cold night had passed and the two lawmen were still inexorably making their way west. The Yellowstone remained on their flank, but not for much longer. The following day they would head up into the foothills, leaving the river to wend its now southerly course down into the territory of Idaho.

The two men, whilst not yet friends in any way, had at least reached an accommodation. They were, after all, fellow lawmen in pursuit of the same objective and so, despite much verbal sparring, they had managed to avoid coming to blows. Bronson was feeling particularly chipper, because he knew something that Bairstow couldn't possibly hope to.

'We'll be living high on the hog this night. Just before the river bends, there's a dwelling made out of prairie marble that'll suit us just fine. It was built by Tector Rawlins and his brother Milo, just after the War Between the States. Sadly they've gone now, just like the big shaggies, but it's the nearest thing to a hotel you'll find in these parts.'

As the Mountie had expected, the 'hotel' proved to be nothing more than a very poor looking cabin fashioned out of sod. It possessed both a chimney and a single door, which directly faced the river some fifty yards away. It could indeed provide shelter for the night, but unfortunately it appeared to be already doing so, because wisps of smoke were emanating from the rudimentary smokestack.

'God damn it to hell,' muttered Bronson angrily. 'The first live people we come across on this trip and it has to be here!'

'Well if they are,' countered Bairstow, 'Then they must have walked here, because I don't see any horses.'

'Unless they're picketed down by the riverbank,' returned the marshal rather too swiftly, because in truth he hadn't immediately noticed the absence of animals.

The other man responded with what he obviously considered to be the coup de grace. 'Allowing any passing Indian the chance to run them off with ease.'

Bronson snorted disdainfully. 'I don't know what kind of Indians you've got up in Canada, but we've civilized ours!'

That statement was so preposterous that the Mountie didn't even trouble to acknowledge it. Instead he angled his mount down towards the river. The pack animal that he was leading grew skittish at the scent of water, rather than from the presence of any other beasts. As they drew closer to the sharp slope leading down to the wide stretch of water, it became obvious that there were no horses concealed there.

'This doesn't smell right at all,' hissed Bronson as he reached for his twelve gauge. 'You stay here with the livestock, while I have a look at that cabin.'

'You just love to give orders don't you, Deputy?' protested the Mountie as he chambered a round into his Winchester.

'That's because I've got jurisdiction, *redcoat*,' Bronson announced peremptorily, before doubling over and making a rush for the cabin. Twenty yards out, he dropped to the ground and silently studied the structure. The wooden door was closed and there were no obvious loopholes in the sod walls. Aiming his shotgun at the door, he drew in a deep breath and bellowed out, 'You in the cabin. I'm a federal officer. Identify yourselves.'

The silence that followed was depressing, because it meant that he would have to do it the hard way, *again*. His missing left hand was itching once more, which was always a bad sign. He tried one more time. 'Open the God damn door or suffer the consequences.'

There was still no answer, so he was left with two choices. Either kick the door in or clamber up on the roof and place his bearskin over the chimney to smoke them out. He shook his head in disgust. This was like a repeat of when they had discovered Thomas. Nobody wanted to say anything.

'Aw shit,' he exclaimed. 'I'm not spoiling a good coat!'

Leaping to his feet, he ran directly for the cabin. Reaching the entrance, he threw himself to one side and then kicked hard at the door. Still no response. Backing off round the corner, the lawman eased out of his heavy coat, which was not simple with a heavy sawn-off and only one hand. Returning to the entrance with the weapon in the crook of his left arm, he hurled the garment into the cabin. The continued silence was making him sweat, but he was now at the point of no return. Gritting his teeth, Bronson stepped cautiously into the single room.

Empty. All that and the poxy cabin was empty! And yet the mystery still remained. A low fire was burning and a huge cauldron of beans was simmering over it. The interior itself was just as he had expected; a hard-packed dirt floor, a per-manently damp earthy smell and the ever-present chance of soil falling from the ceiling. Up against the walls, there were two very rudimentary wood framed cots, lacking both mat-tress and blankets. In short, there was nothing to confirm human occupation . . . other than the fire and the food.

Cursing fluently, Bronson turned to the door. It was then that he heard the drumming hoof beats. From the sound of them, there was a sizeable party and they were in a hurry. Maybe they thought that the beans were burning!

'Jesus Christ, what a mess,' he snarled in exasperation. Through the open door he could see Bairstow poised to come running. Such action would be certain to give away their presence and leave them both trapped in the cabin, so he frantically gestured for the Mountie to stay where he was. The horsemen were closing fast. There was nothing to do but shut the flimsy door and wait. It was attached to its frame by some very worn leather straps. By tugging on it, he was able to wedge it in the earth so that he could just see out. Bronson stood there and fumed. Things really hadn't panned out as expected.

As the riders pounded up to the cabin, several things happened in quick succession. The vibrations brought down a shower of earth on to the lawman's head, which certainly didn't improve his temper. Then there was much shouting outside, as though an argument was in progress and it was at that point Bronson recognized one of the horsemen!

With his mind turning somersaults, the marshal shook the dirt from his hair and feverishly considered his options. He now knew for certain that the newcomers were living outside of the law *and* were most definitely hostile. From the look of some of the others, they were most likely unwelcome visitors from Canada. There were simply too many of them for tenancy of the cabin to be settled peacefully and a prior challenge was out of the question. Praying that the Mountie would keep his cool, Bronson backed away from the door into shadow and waited.

With a gentle bubbling coming from the fireplace, it occurred to him that he would far rather feed them than fight them. One thing was for sure; he did not relish discharging his big gun in such a confined space, but knew that he had no other choice. With both hammers cocked, he held the weapon at waist height to mitigate the concussion and listened intently as the men dismounted. There was a heated ongoing discussion, some of it in heavily accented and pigeon English, concerning the transport of something.

'I don't like steamboats or rafts or any damn thing that floats,' whined one of the men. 'They always blow up or sink.'

'So swim then,' came the caustic response and then finally one of them got around to opening the door.

A heavily-bearded individual wearing buckskins strolled nonchalantly into the cabin. He was in the process of hurling a casual insult over his shoulder. As his glance fell on the bulky lawman and then the gaping muzzles of the sawn-off, his jaw froze in shock. Behind him two more men crowded in, drawn by the aroma of hot food. Bronson braced himself against the mayhem and squeezed both triggers. The resulting roar seemed to fill the room as the twin loads of shot engulfed the three men.

CHAPTER FIVE

Even some fifty yards away, the crashing detonation made Bairstow jump with surprise. In the cabin's threshold, three men tumbled to the ground beneath a cloud of powder smoke. One lay perfectly still, whilst the other two twitched uncontrollably. There had been no warning of any kind. Louis Riel's supporters were unlikely to be the only French Canadians south of the border, so how on earth did the marshal know for certain that this group were hostile? One thing was for sure. If they weren't before, they definitely would be now!

Reacting fast, the Mountie levelled his Winchester. Because he was in direct line of sight with the cabin, he had to aim low. A bullet coming out of a 45/70 cartridge could easily punch through the target and on into Bronson. His meaty shoulder absorbed the powerful recoil as his first shot rang out. Even through the thin veil of smoke, he could clearly see his victim spin round and drop. The bullet had caught that unfortunate in the right thigh.

The remaining men rapidly came to their senses and began discharging their side arms. A fusillade of wild shots rang out. Earth and stones were kicked up around Bairstow's position. The golden rule in such situations was to fire and move. Ducking down behind the riverbank, he levered in another cartridge and then dashed a few paces to his left.

In the smoke-filled cabin, Bronson had drawn his Remington and then dropped to the floor. A thin trickle of blood came from his right ear, sure sign of a perforated eardrum. He didn't hear Bairstow's shot, but he saw the man outside fall and then the others return fire. At least the damned Mountie knew how to bring a man down. Gagging against the bile rising in his throat, he took aim at a broad back and fired.

From his new position by the river, the Canadian loosed off another shot. Simultaneously another weapon discharged in the cabin. Its victim gasped in shock and collapsed to the ground. The dwindling group of men abruptly realized that their situation was untenable. As Nelson Pruitt gazed around in wide-eyed shock, a frighteningly familiar voice cried out from the cabin.

'Federal officers. Drop your weapons and get down in the dirt!'

'Holy shit!' howled Pruitt in abject horror. 'It's that bastard marshal.' With that, he pointed his revolver at the doorway and frantically fanned the hammer until inevitably the weapon dry-fired. Such wild shooting rarely succeeded and he knew that his only chance of survival against Bronson was to again run like hell.

'Let's get the hell out of here,' he bellowed. He didn't give a damn about the others, but he knew that with them all milling about around him he stood more chance.

The remaining men didn't need telling twice. Those that could ran for their horses. The animals were crazed with fear and it took a deal of whipping and cursing before the fugitives were mounted. Bairstow sighted down on a rearing beast and squeezed the trigger. Whinnying with pain, the horse slewed sideways before managing to right itself. It then took off at speed with its rider clinging on for dear life. The Mountie recognized the fact that they would now have another blood trail to follow if they so chose.

Four other men managed to escape the killing ground. Included in their number was Nelson Pruitt. Even as he charged across the frozen prairie, he was trying to work out just how that damned lawman had managed to find him again. Was it pure chance *or* was he after the Canadians? One thing was for sure. They would meet again, if only because Nelson had a personal score to settle over the death of his brother.

Only when the survivors were safely out of range did Bairstow emerge from cover. He levered in another cartridge and cautiously advanced towards the cabin. There had been a great deal of violence in a very short space of time. Of the five casualties, only one appeared likely to last the night, but where was the marshal?

'Bronson, are you still drawing breath?'

The lack of response brought a chill to his bones. In spite of their early differences, the prospect of losing his companion so soon did not appeal. Apart from anything else, the manhunt would almost certainly have to be postponed, as he did not know the country. Reaching the luckless individual that he had wounded, the Mountie kicked away the man's revolver and then, ignoring his cries for help, gingerly approached the threshold. Although only one of the victims of the double shotgun blast was actually dead, the other two appeared past help and therefore apparently presented no threat. Bairstow's only thoughts were focused on the

American and so he was thus dangerously preoccupied. Fearing for the worst, he finally stepped into the cabin.

The sight that met his eyes beggared all belief. Rather than lying stricken from a stray bullet, the marshal was eagerly spooning beans into his mouth. The hot juice from them coated his moustache and trickled down his chin. He appeared to be completely oblivious to the carnage outside.

'Well that just beats all,' commented the Mountie scathingly. 'You've just gunned down four men and all you want to do is eat.'

Bronson's only response was to continue feeding. He did not even have the decency to greet his companion.

'For Christ's sake,' bellowed the Mountie. 'Are you deaf?'

Bronson jerked in surprise and abruptly turned to face him. There was a dreamily distant look in his eyes that suggested that he wasn't quite himself. 'You might have to shout,' he remarked mildly. 'I think I may be deaf.'

Bairstow noticed the blood on the side of the other man's face and sighed apologetically. His embarrassed understanding suddenly turned to horrified confusion as Bronson's serene expression abruptly contorted into one of concentrated fury. In one fluid movement the marshal discarded the dripping spoon, drew and cocked his Remington and fired. From the doorway, there came an agonized scream and another shot. As a bullet smacked harmlessly into the nearby sod wall, Bronson fired again. As the Mountie twisted round, he was just in time to see a blood spattered survivor of the shotgun blast take a second bullet in the chest. With his own ears ringing painfully, he moved swiftly over to the other two apparently dead men. They were both drenched in blood and gore from multiple wounds, but this time Bairstow took no chances. Unwilling to waste any cartridges, he kicked them hard and repeatedly in the ribs until he was sure that they were not playing possum. Feeling guilty at having overlooked them in the first place, he chose not to return to the cabin, but instead advanced on the only man left alive.

Having witnessed the renewed violence, that man had fallen silent, but there was no doubt that he was in serious pain. His sallow features had turned white with shock, whilst his bloodshot eyes were as wide as saucers. From the position of his right leg, it was obvious that Bairstow's high-powered bullet had shattered the bone. In such conditions, his chances of survival were slim.

Brutalized by years on the frontier, the Mountie had no scruples about taking advantage of the situation. With his fur-covered boot, he none-too-gently nudged the outlaw's damaged leg. The man's response was instantaneous. He flinched with pain and fear and began to drag himself away. 'What do you want with me?' he wailed in barely intelligible English. 'I have done nothing to you. I don't even know you.'

Bairstow favoured him with a half-smile. Unfastening his buffalo coat, he opened it with a flourish, so revealing the bright red jacket beneath. 'I'll wager that you recognize this though,' he responded grimly.

Surprise briefly supplanted pain in the half-breed's eyes. He obviously believed that he had left the hated Mounted Police far behind when he fled south.

'We know where Labeau is,' continued his inquisitor. 'But what brings you here with that American?'

Bronson came out of the cabin. Bairstow could hear the click-click-click of a revolver cylinder as the marshal replaced the empty cartridges, but he kept his eyes firmly focused on the Metis. That man obviously possessed a modicum of intelligence, because apparent understanding suddenly registered on his face. His eyes flitted back and forth between the two men looming over him.

'Whether I answer your questions or not, you're just going to leave me out here to die!'

'Rubbish,' barked Bronson, whose hearing was obviously returning. 'You're not in Canada now. I carry the law in these parts. We'll splint your leg and put you on a horse. You can even have your fill of those beans before you go. Just tell me about your business with Nelson Pruitt and you're a free man.'

The Metis, who had known only privation in his short life, took in the hard eyes and ready weapons and instinctively knew that the best he could hope for was a quick end, rather than the long and lingering death that was really in prospect. He rapidly came to a chillingly practical decision. Ignoring the gut wrenching pain in his leg, he twisted away from the two men and lunged for the nearest discarded weapon. Even as his hand closed over a revolver butt, there came a loud report from Bairstow's Winchester. The bullet struck him in the back of his head, which seemed to explode like a ripe melon. The man's life was snuffed out in an instant.

Bronson shook his head in disbelief. 'That was one hell of a brave son of a bitch. If they're all like him over at Alder Gulch, we could have a problem!'

Nelson Pruitt seethed with almost ungovernable rage. The more that he thought about Jesse Bronson, the more he itched to turn about and settle things there and then. Strangely, his courage seemed to increase in direct proportion to the distance that he put between himself and the cabin. It was the death of the wounded horse that brought him back to his senses. As the animal collapsed, its rider fell heavily and lay winded on the hard ground. The other three Metis horsemen reined in and waited impatiently while their comrade recovered. They were gravely unsettled by the unprovoked attack and were nervous as to how to explain their defeat to Labeau. It was lucky for Pruitt that they did not realize that he was at least partially to blame.

While they were all sat there, the American came to a decision. There was altogether too much money to be made out of Labeau's temporary occupation of Alder Gulch for the outlaw to simply cut and run. The Metis leader controlled the camp, but did not have the contacts needed to dispose of the gold. He needed the Yankee brigand for that. Yet for all the men and guns available to Labeau, Pruitt feared that the arrival of a federal marshal could upset everything.

That particular poxy lawman seemed to have nine lives and he was no longer alone. His presence could pull together the cowed miners. What Pruitt needed was reliable help. Just like he had had before Taylor got shot to pieces at Fallowfield's. Someone who knew how to fight mean and who would take on any number of lawmen if there was money in it. Someone permanently angry, but whose limited intelligence would not prove a threat to that of Nelson's.

As the dismounted Metis climbed up behind one of his companions, Pruitt announced his plans. He explained away his recognition of the marshal and told them of his suspicion that the lawmen were heading for the mining camp. There were men available who would be happy to take on any amount of law and he was heading off to get them.

The French Canadians were plainly dubious about his intended departure, but were under instructions not to harm the American. They had also just lost five comrades to the lawmen, in addition to the two killed earlier by Thomas Cates and so could not doubt the danger approaching from the east. It was with mixed feelings then that they watched him ride off at speed. More than one of them wished that they were going along, as above all else they dreaded Labeau's reaction when only four men returned minus the all-important American.

It was late the following afternoon when Jacques Labeau finally decided to make his move. Most of the camp's occupants were at the diggings or panning for flake under the watchful eyes of his own men. The mental vision of Kirsty Lander's trim yet voluptuous figure had been eating at him for days. Mere greed could no longer keep a check on his lust. It was a sad fact that he hadn't enjoyed a woman since fleeing Batoche at the close of the rebellion, so even the cold couldn't dampen his ardour. Besides, he was from Canada and well used to such conditions.

After briskly rubbing a grubby forefinger over his yellow teeth, Labeau splashed some water over his greasy hair. Using his fingers as a comb, he dragged his unkempt mane into some sort of order. He was in the cabin that he had appropriated upon their arrival. The miner had obviously had a woman, because there was a small cracked mirror near the bed. Peering into it, Labeau admired his manly reflection. He told himself that any woman would welcome his attentions and if she didn't, then so much the worse for her. The half-breed also happened to have a skinning knife concealed in his right boot, just in case any persuasion should be required. His heart beat even faster at the thought that he might just need to use it. Barely able to control his excitement, he leapt to his feet and strode to the door.

Kirsty gently mopped the sweat on her father's brow. He had a high fever, brought on by infection in the wound and was periodically emitting violent bursts of incoherent ravings. The realization that his condition was deteriorating and that he was likely to die had placed her in a state of acute mental turmoil. If his death now appeared certain, then why not take the risk of extracting the bullet and anything else that was in the wound? Heavily dosed with laudanum, he was unlikely to suffer overmuch and the only worst-case scenario was that he might meet his maker that bit sooner. Dreading what had to be done, she decided to enlist Deckard Foster's help when he returned from the diggings.

The creaking of the shack door behind her caught Kirsty's attention. Thinking that it must be one of the few other women in the camp, she turned to offer a weary greeting. Her heart jumped with shock when she saw the menacing individual standing in the doorway. Worn down by anxiety, she did not immediately recognize what his presence signified. It was only as the swarthy figure advanced on her that she belatedly realized what he was after.

'Don't look so shocked, my pretty,' Labeau remarked softly. 'You knew I would come for you eventually.' As he spoke, he eased out of his heavy coat and casually let it fall to the floor. Then his rabid glance took in her father on the only bed and he registered momentary confusion. Not having slept properly for days, he had forgotten all about the damned old troublemaker. Labeau's temples throbbed and there was an insistent ache in his groin that just had to be relieved.

'Get away from here,' she snapped. 'You've brought enough suffering to this family!'

Moving rapidly into the room, he seized her arms and hissed, 'Come with me to my cabin now, or I'll heave the old fool on to the floor and take you here in front of him. Which will it be?'

Kirsty stared up at his frenzied features and knew that it wasn't a bluff. Labeau was sweating as much as her father, only his fever was of a different kind. Feeling the immense power in his grip, she realized that her only chance was to play along. Lowering her head in apparent subservience, she mumbled, 'I'll go with you. Just don't touch him, please.'

Encouraged by that response, Labeau grunted and took her wrist. Bounding out of the shack, his eagerness was such that he almost dragged her off her feet. Desperately she looked around the camp for help. The winding mud churned street was bordered on both sides by many wooden buildings, but there was just no one in sight except the guards manning the Gatling gun and she knew it was pointless to look to them for help. They would more than likely wish to join in.

And then they were in his cabin. With an animal like snarl, her captor threw Kirsty across the room on to the wooden frame bed. Slamming the door, he drew in a deep breath and then moved in on her like a big cat.

'I'm going to enjoy this,' he slavered. 'And hard or easy, so are you!'

She knew that she would only get the one chance to make a break for it. Timing was everything. Forcing herself to relax, she fixed her eyes on his and lay back on the soiled sheets. Slowly, as though reluctantly accepting the inevitable, the young woman gave a deep sigh and sensuously raised her shapely legs. Appreciating the apparent change in her demeanour, a dreamy look came over Labeau as he approached the bed and began to unbutton his trousers.

At the very moment that a set of grubby long johns was unveiled, there came a pounding of hoofs out on the street and Kirsty kicked out with all her strength. The Canadian may have been pre-occupied, but he was still able to react to the sudden assault. Twisting like a snake, he was just able to protect his groin. Even so, Kirsty's feet struck his left hip with tremendous force and sent him tumbling back to the floor.

Outside, familiar voices called out to the men by the Gatling gun enquiring after their leader's whereabouts. A jocular answer was forthcoming and then someone approached the cabin. As a heavy fist pounded on the door, there came a cry of, 'Jacques, are you in there?'

Wincing with pain, Labeau levered himself on to all fours and spat on the floorboards. 'By Christ, they pick their time,' he snarled as his maddened eyes settled on hers. Drawing his knife from its hidden scabbard, he called out in a louder voice, 'What is it? What do you want?'

The voice outside sounded confused. 'We have news. There are things that you should know.'

'Oh, can't it wait,' howled their leader petulantly. 'I am . . . busy just now!'

There was a short silence beyond the door. Then the speaker, more nervous this time, replied in a rush. 'There's a U S Marshal on our back trail and he's not alone. They ambushed us down by the Yellowstone. We lost five men and

I reckon they'll fetch up here. Pruitt's gone for help.'

Labeau froze, the knife in his hand temporarily forgotten. Frenzy of a different kind was starting to build within him. Myriad thoughts burst forth in his overheated mind. 'Marshals work for the government. How could they know where we are? I need Pruitt here to help in selling the gold. And just what kind of *help* has he gone for?' He groaned with a frustration that was no longer purely sexual.

As Kirsty recognized his preoccupation, she leapt from the bed and raced for the door. Just as she reached it, it was cautiously opened by one of his Metis followers. That man took in her presence and Labeau's position on the floor and gulped hesitantly.

'By Christ,' screamed the rebel leader. 'Can't I even rape a woman in peace?'

In the face of such concentrated fury, the Metis took a step back and it was all that Kirsty needed. Throwing herself through the startled group, she raced off down the muddy street. Even as she ran, the scared but determined young lady realized that she now had no option other than to leave the settlement.

CHAPTER SIX

'You realize we've lost the advantage of surprise, don't you?'

The two lawmen were working their way up through the foothills towards the mining camp. Well beyond that lay the Rocky Mountains, which no man in his right mind would venture into in winter. They had spent a reasonably comfortable night protected from the elements in the cabin, gorging on the hot beans and coffee that had been so conveniently provided for them. The five blood spattered cadavers had been left in a neat row, as though by way of a tasteless joke, for whatever creatures that chanced to find them. After all, the bodies represented little monetary value even in trade, except possibly for their teeth, and the ground was far too hard for a mass burial to be considered.

It seemed, after a full day's riding, that the Yellowstone River was merely a distant memory. The Mountie had been pondering on their situation and he wasn't happy, hence his sour comment.

Bronson casually spat out a disgusting stream of tobacco juice, before regarding him speculatively. 'I thought you redcoats thrived on going it alone. The thin red line and all that shit!'

Bairstow favoured him with a scornful glance. The collars of his thick buffalo coat were pulled up around his heavily bearded features. The temperature had dropped noticeably since they had moved up into the hills. 'You know damned well that we are heavily outnumbered. We could be riding into a trap right now.'

Even as he said this, his eyes roamed restlessly over the unfamiliar terrain. Encumbered as they were with pack mules, they would make a prime target for an ambuscade. The trees and rocks could have easily concealed any number of Labeau's followers. He felt uneasy and did not enjoy being dependent upon the American's local knowledge.

When his companion did respond, however, his earlier bantering tone had gone, replaced by one of cool considered logic. 'Yes, they know we're coming, but not exactly where from. We're keeping well clear of any recognized trails, which is one reason why the going is getting harder. Even if Pruitt is working with Labeau, you can be sure *he* won't be wandering around these hills looking for us. Remember, I know that little shit of old. He's a back-shooter at heart and so will keep clear of trouble for as long as he can. I believe that the most your man will do is send out a few scouts to try and spot our approach. If they have got a Gatling gun, they'll likely place a lot of store by it, but you can't run around a hillside with one of those things. So I reckon those cockchafers will stay close to Alder Gulch and wait on events.'

Bronson then favoured his companion with a shrewd glance before asking, 'Was that a measured enough response for you?' As the Mountie registered surprise at such eloquence he added, 'My ma made sure I did my letters and ciphers at a Quaker school. It kind of throws some folk.'

Bairstow could not resist a wry smile, before the lurking knowledge of what they were up against, once more darkened his expression. 'I just think we're badly overmatched is all. We could use some help with this.'

'Be careful what you wish for,' the marshal responded cryptically.

Kirsty's face was pale but determined as she locked stares with Deckard Foster.

'If a federal marshal is on his way here,' she declared, 'Then Thomas must have got through. Which means there might be a doctor with him.'

The burly enforcer was dubious. 'There's no way Cates could have got all the way to Billings and then back with help so quickly. It just isn't possible. Besides, what can one lone marshal do against this gang of cutthroats?'

'He's not alone,' Kirsty persisted stubbornly. 'Labeau's men said he had help. Enough for him to kill five of the Metis. That's got to count for something!'

'That's as maybe,' allowed Foster. 'But that bastard must have close on thirty men left, not to mention that damned Gatling. How can they sneak in here, past Labeau's guards and surprise them all?'

What Kirsty said next stunned the older man. Lowering her voice, she replied, 'Because I'm going out there to find them and lead them back in here, that's how. I can't stay here after what just happened. Once Labeau gets organized he'll come looking for me again and you know it!'

Before Foster could protest, the embittered young woman continued remorselessly. 'That God damned son of a bitch had my father shot, and nearly raped me. I'm going to make him pay and. . . .' As she momentarily hesitated, tears came to her eyes. 'And if there is a sawbones out there, he can dig that bullet out of Pa, otherwise we'll have to do it!'

Foster saw the mixture of anguish and determination on her lovely face and knew that he had no chance of talking her out of it.

Dutch Henry Bruckner glowered menacingly at the group of prospectors as they cheerfully savoured their first whiskey of the day. Partial to all and any type of alcohol that hadn't been previously swallowed, he had been drinking the house gut rot slowly and steadily for the entire afternoon, pausing only to take on board a tin plate full of greasy bacon and beans. In a country of legendary boozers, he could hold his own with the best and would have been viewed with outright despair by any representative of the American Temperance Society.

His mood was unstable on the best of occasions, but by the time a lack of light had brought an end to the working day, his humour had turned dark and ugly. As the harsh liquid trickled down his throat, his jaw tightened and his left eye began to twitch uncontrollably. None of the noisy gang had even glanced his way, but something about their jovial mood had triggered a perverse resentment. Maybe it was because it was such a long time since he had had anything to be genuinely happy about.

The barkeeper easily recognized the signs. He had been working at the saloon in White Sulphur Springs, Montana since it had first opened for business and knew all the regulars thereabouts. Mostly they were decent folks, but a small minority were just plain mean. So it was that periodically his right hand would reassuringly caress the butt of the sawn-off that he kept under the counter. He jovially referred to it as his 'crowd pleaser', when in fact it was anything but. Not that he had any intention of using it unless his own life was under threat. Nobody in their right mind would wave anything in front of Dutch Henry, unless they seriously intended to kill him stone dead and then permanently leave town ahead of pursuit by his cronies.

The fact that he was seriously outnumbered did not worry the solitary brooding drinker one jot. In fact, he didn't even give it a thought. At more than six and a half feet tall, he was an absolute beast of a man. His shoulders were like house sides and he possessed hands like hams. He had been at various times a logger, coal miner and slaughterman. Then he discovered crime and found it far more to his liking. For the moment, however, he was vaguely awaiting the next job and welcomed a brawl between equals: which is how he viewed odds of eight to one. And it seemed to be up to him to open the proceedings.

'I've had enough of listening to you bunch of pricks,' he announced with a booming voice that was only slightly slurred.

Silence descended on the room and then a number of things happened at once. The barkeeper began to remove anything breakable from the counter and all the other patrons headed for the swing doors, with the exception of the eight prospectors. They, confident in their numbers, merely turned to peer curiously over at him. All of them knew Dutch Henry by sight. It was said that he had no more smile than a turnip, but they were all strong capable individuals and none of them had had the benefit of observing him in action. However, it did suddenly occur to one of them that it might after all be best to humour the big fellow.

'We surely didn't mean to upset you, Dutch,' offered the spokesman. 'We surely didn't. Here, have another joy juice on us.'

The huge man reared up like an angry bear. 'You snivelling piece of puke,' he roared. 'I buy my own drinks. I've got money, see.' With that, he kicked away his upturned table and lumbered towards the group at the bar. That he was liquored up was not in doubt, but it certainly hadn't affected his perception. 'You touch that sawn-off, Kent,' he snarled, 'and it'll be the last thing you do on this earth.'

The barkeeper jerked involuntarily at the casual, yet oh so lethal, threat and then backed slowly away. Other than belt knives, the prospectors were all unarmed. With the remaining Indians no longer considered much of a menace, very few of the miners bothered to carry firearms. Dutch Henry had a huge Colt Dragoon tucked into his belt, but showed no inclination to draw it. He only carried such an out-dated piece because he considered its very size to be intimidating, just like himself.

Drawing up in front of the men, the solitary antagonist peered down at the one who had offered to buy him a drink. 'Looks like you're first in line for a slap, little man.'

That individual answered reasonably, but with a noticeable air of desperation. 'I meant no offence, Dutch. We don't want any trouble.'

Dutch Henry glowered down at the nervous creature and offered a snippet of advice. 'What you want and what you get don't always match up.'

So saying, he abruptly grabbed hold of the prospector by his throat and left thigh. With a gut-wrenching effort, the big man lifted him bodily from the floor until that choking unfortunate was literally horizontal. With the veins in his bull-like neck bulging from the strain, Dutch Henry then turned and tossed his helpless victim at the nearest miners. They had formed a semi-circle around their giant tormentor and with the bar behind them had nowhere to run. The dead weight of their friend crashed into three of them, crushing them against the solid timber counter. All of them collapsed to the floor in varying degrees of distress.

The remaining four men were suddenly no longer interested in conciliatory gestures. One of them grabbed their nearly full whiskey bottle from the counter, upended it and viciously smashed it over Dutch Henry's head. If he had expected such a stunning blow to topple the giant, he was in for a rude awakening. With whiskey and shards of glass clinging to his greasy matted hair, that man merely rotated his thick neck to better view his assailant. Nodding, as if with derision, Dutch Henry lashed out with a tremendous backhanded slap, which literally lifted his victim off his feet. As the man tumbled back against the unyielding bar counter, the back of his head struck the edge and he slumped to the floor as though pole-axed.

That meant that five men were now out of the amazingly one-sided fight, but the remaining revellers had abruptly realized just what they were up against and had started to use their brains. As one man threw a chair at Dutch Henry's legs, the other two hurled themselves bodily at him. As their combined weight struck him, he got tangled up in the furniture and fell backwards. With a shattering thump that ejected all the air in his lungs, he struck the floorboards full-length and lay there with whiskey dripping off his nose and chin.

What the three men should have done at that point was

skedaddle, but one of them just couldn't resist taking a swing at the fallen leviathan. With his two companions pinning Dutch Henry's arms, he planted a scything blow on the helpless man's nose. With a roar of pain and outrage, that man sucked in a great draught of air. With renewed strength, he suddenly contracted his outstretched limbs and slammed the two prospectors together. Their heads connected with a sickening crunch and they were abruptly out of the fight. With the bar room brawl suddenly reduced to one-on-one, Dutch Henry clambered to his feet and ruefully fingered his mangled snout.

'You shouldn't have done that,' he mumbled menacingly at the last man standing. Swiftly grabbing that mesmerized unfortunate by his shirtfront, he swung a massive fist that launched his victim into and then over the counter. The senseless body landed at the feet of the aggrieved barkeeper.

'Jesus, Dutch,' protested Kent unhappily. 'Why did you have to go and do that? They were good customers.'

That man shook his head and then gazed over at him, as though peering through a fog. 'Because they looked too damned happy, that's why!'

Kent leaned over the counter and mournfully scrutinized the devastation. Tables and chairs were shattered and there was more than a little blood to be scrubbed from the floorboards. Those men who were still conscious had the wit to stay down and were waiting to see what their massive assailant's next move would be. It was at that very moment that the door opened and a great blast of chilled air blew in.

Nelson Pruitt was cold, dog-tired and desperate for a shot of whiskey. He had spent all day riding into the teeth of a bitter north wind. White Sulphur Springs did not amount to much, but after such a journey it seemed like heaven. He was eagerly looking forward to a drink, a bath and a whore – in that order. The extensive display of carnage in the bar was not at all what he had expected, but then his weary eyes took in the massive figure of Dutch Henry Bruckner and all became clear.

'Hot dang, Dutch,' Pruitt drawled. 'Looks like you've been having a celebration.'

A pair of red-rimmed, watering eyes fastened on the new-comer. Recognition dawned and very gradually the hint of what might just have passed for a smile spread across the big man's brutalized features.

'Nelson Pruitt, you little shit!' he exclaimed generously. 'Didn't expect to see you around these parts. Heard tell your big brother got cut in two by a sawn-off over at Fallowfield's.'

Pruitt grimaced at the raw memory and suddenly had to work hard at maintaining an affable demeanour. 'I've got a proposition to put to you. One that might place some money in your pocket *and* give us the chance to settle matters with a certain Marshal Bronson, but we'll need some help.'

Dutch Henry regarded the other man closely for long moments before nodding slowly. He too had good reason to hate the lawman and it involved some very hard time served in a federal penitentiary.

'If truth be told, I was getting a bit bored round here,' he remarked, to a collective sigh of relief in the bar, before waving the new arrival over to a table.

Pruitt gratefully sat down opposite and drew in a deep breath. Puzzlingly the whole area absolutely reeked of whiskey, far more than would be expected even in a frontier bar room. The outlaw discreetly scrutinized the monster of

63

a man sitting before him. That individual's hair appeared to be soaking and there were bits of glass glinting in it. In all innocence, he enquired, 'You been drinking, Dutch?'

CHAPTER SEVEN

The two lawmen had passed a desperately cold and uncomfortable night in amongst a jumble of boulders and trees. There had been no question of lighting even a small fire, so the dreaded phrase cold camp took on a literal meaning. With the first tentative light of dawn, they gratefully scrambled out of their frost-covered blankets and stamped about to get the circulation moving.

'I'm getting too old for this,' muttered Bronson in all seriousness. His right hip ached, as though from the onset of rheumatism and all his fingers were stiff, even inside thick gloves.

'This is nothing,' responded his younger companion amiably. 'Back home in the higher latitudes, I've gone through winters where it was so cold that the air itself froze!'

Bronson groaned at yet another tall tale from the Mountie and yet unusually for him he really couldn't think of a good put down. It was simply just *too* bitter!

They were negotiating the treacherous terrain on foot, leading their four animals behind them, when Bairstow abruptly flung up his arm. The two men dropped to the hard ground, Winchesters at the ready.

'What is it?' hissed the marshal. 'What have you seen?' He was more than a little peeved that *he* hadn't spotted whatever was out there. There was a momentary silence before his companion answered.

'There was something moving amongst the trees. A flash of white. I don't think it was a beast.'

Bronson came to a swift decision. He might not have seen it, but he'd sure as hell catch it. 'Wait here with the animals while I go look.'

Without giving the Mountie chance to object, he eased out from behind his boulder and moved off up the hill. He angled off to the right, so as to come around and then behind whatever was up there. Jesse Bronson was no light-weight, but he could be very quiet on his feet when he needed to. Moving steadily uphill, he crept from tree to tree, utilizing the natural cover as best he could.

So it was that after a time, he came out above and to the side of a small hunched figure. The white apparel that had caught Bairstow's eye appeared to be a scarf or some form of headgear. Either way, it seemed a strange choice for someone who was attempting to remain hidden.

The marshal was just about to close in, when something else caught his attention. The individual before him had failed to spot his approach because of a prior interest. A little further round the hillside was another observer; only this one was gazing back down the slope, as though seeking to detect and ambush unwary travellers. Or, just maybe, a couple of unwelcome peace officers!

It was then that Bronson decided to proceed purely on the basis of a hunch. Something told him that the nearest individual didn't present any danger to them. So keeping his

Winchester in the crook of his left arm, he moved forward slowly and carefully. Every step brought him nearer to the unsuspecting person. Then the inevitable happened. His right boot came down on a dry twig and the spy twisted around in horrified alarm.

Remarkably it was a woman, and quite obviously a pretty one, even with her face partially concealed by a scarf. Without hesitation she drew a knife from under her thick coat. That she was frightened was obvious, but there was also fire in her eyes *and* thankfully she had the sense to remain silent. With normal speech impossible, he did the only thing remaining to him. Very slowly he drew back his buffalo coat, so as to display his well-worn badge of office.

Kirsty's eyes locked on to it, flitted over to his missing left hand and then back to the badge. Her relief was obvious and as the tension drained from both of them, he favoured her with a genuine smile. Then he motioned for her to move closer, to allow a whispered conversation. She complied without hesitation and in so doing demonstrated that she was nimble and sure-footed on the broken terrain.

'You waiting for me, little lady?' he murmured.

'If you're the marshal from Billings,' she responded instantly.

'I am he.' Briefly taking his eyes from her, he nodded over at the distant figure. 'Are there any more of him lurking around these parts?'

'Not between here and Alder Gulch that I know of, but then I've never done this sort of thing before,' Kirsty openly admitted. Then her eyes narrowed as she put the question. 'You going to kill him now?'

'I reckon not,' he responded solemnly. That she was eager for some bloodletting was plain to see and he pondered briefly on the cause. For her to be out on the hillside unaccompanied, suggested that things were going badly in the mining camp. 'Dime to a dollar, he's not alone out here. Any shooting will alert his *compadres*, so we'll leave him still breathing and none the wiser.'

With that, he turned and began to retrace his steps. Gratefully, he heard her following on, because there could be no place for an argument within earshot of an enemy.

It was only when Kirsty and the marshal joined Bairstow that she realized the true size of the relief party. 'Are you all there is?' she exclaimed in horror. 'Where's the doctor? Didn't Thomas tell you about my pa?'

'It was just luck that we found him near to death on the trail,' explained Bronson. 'Those half-breeds had caught up with him before he got anywhere near Billings. I'd already been assigned to track them down, but we didn't know their whereabouts until we heard it from your man.'

Kirsty's frustration was obvious. 'And who the hell's this?' she demanded, indicating the Mountie.

'That's Canada's answer to a peace officer,' replied Bronson with a wry smile.

That man strode eagerly forward to introduce himself. He had already carried out a full inspection of the young lady and had come to the rapid conclusion that she was undeniably attractive.

'Corporal Samuel Bairstow of the North West Mounted Police, ma'am. Or is it possibly Miss?'

'Oh, for pity's sake,' groaned Bronson. 'We haven't got time for sweet niceties. We need to keep moving on to the camp before any of Labeau's scouts trip over us. You can take point and lead us in,' he instructed Kirsty. 'But first you'd better tell us just what's been going on in Alder Gulch. Oh and get rid of that damn scarf. It's far too bright for skulking.'

Her response was unequivocal. 'My ma gave me this on her death bed. I never travel without it and I'm not going to start now. Besides, you wouldn't have found me without it!'

The Mountie chuckled appreciatively. She was a real firebrand and none the worse for it.

By the time the three of them had reached the outskirts of the camp, both men knew all of relevance that had taken place in Alder Gulch since Labeau's half-breeds had sprung upon it. They learnt of the initial deaths amongst Deckard Foster's men, of the shooting of Kirsty's father and of her own very personal harassment at the hands of the Metis leader. Every word that Kirsty uttered demonstrated her anger at, and loathing of, the intruders. She left them in no doubt as to how she wished matters to proceed.

'If you can get hold of that big gun, you could slaughter them all!'

Even in such pressured circumstances, Bairstow found himself physically attracted to the firebrand, but the marshal had other thoughts on his mind. 'There may well be killing,' he allowed. 'But I'm not looking for a massacre! They want to see prisoners back over the border, not a pile of cadavers. So we need to survey the layout and make a plan.'

Kirsty was adamant on one score. 'And we need to see to my pa.'

With the animals ground tethered out of sight, she led the lawmen to a hidden vantage point on the side of the ravine overlooking the main thoroughfare. Alder Gulch had sprung into vigorous life over twenty years earlier and the population had been so sizeable that for a while some people had even lived in dugouts and under overhanging rocks. Over time the main gold deposits had played out and the bulk of the opportunists moved on, but there was still enough flake to be panned and enough ore to be dug up to keep the camp viable. Log cabins served to keep the bitter cold out and gave the settlement a feeling of permanence.

The two lawmen viewed the street below them with practised eyes. The obvious strongpoint was the Gatling gun with its three attendants. That had to be neutralized first if they were to have any chance of relieving the camp. Such a task would be easier to achieve after dark, but was impractical because the workforce would have returned by then and might easily get caught up in any wild shooting.

'It ain't going to be easy getting the drop on those fellows,' muttered Bronson as he viewed the muffled individuals pacing around by the gun. 'They look like they're on hot bricks.'

'Labeau put the fear of God into them after he sent out the scouts,' Kirsty responded bitterly. She knew to her cost exactly what happened to those that displeased the Metis leader.

Bairstow was unusually silent as he pondered the problem. An idea had occurred to him, but it represented one hell of a risk. It was the sheer determination on Kirsty's highly attractive features that finally convinced him to try it. She had displayed great spirit and with any luck might just favourably recognize that same quality in someone else. Leaning over to the marshal, he announced gravely, 'I'll be your diversion. It'll give you the chance to take out that gun. Just don't mess it up, that's all!'

*

The three guards were consumed by conflicting emotions. They were proud at having been entrusted with the awesome firepower of the big gun and yet they were so cold that they had lost feeling in their feet. Because they were under ferocious instructions to remain with the Gatling at all times, all they could do was stomp manically about in a semi-circle. Perversely, they were actually looking forward to darkness falling, because they could then at least huddle around the pitch torches. The guards were also nervous. They had heard talk of the approach of a United States marshal. They did not know exactly what one of those was, but it was said that he had killed many of their comrades sent out in pursuit of the miner. Such a man must possess a great deal of power!

The vision in scarlet that suddenly appeared at the other end of the street totally transfixed them all. He wore the uniform of the hated Canadian Police, but surely no single redcoat would dare enter Alder Gulch alone. Such an awesome display of confidence could only come from having many men at his back.

Despite having discarded his buffalo coat in such bitter cold, the Mountie's body was damp with sweat. He nervously sat astride his horse in the centre of the street, expecting to feel the crushing blow of a bullet at any moment.

After apprehensively clearing his throat, he got a grip of his fears and managed to bellow out forcefully, 'My name is Corporal Samuel Bairstow of the North West Mounted Police. Your camp is completely surrounded. You *will* lay down your weapons at once or rivers of blood will flow!'

The three men fingered their guns uneasily. No one had yet reached for the Gatling, because they were overwhelmed by indecision. They could still only see one man, but what if there was truth in his words? At that very moment there could be any number of rifles aimed directly at them!

Inside the adjacent cabin, Jacques Labeau jerked upright at the peremptory command. After failing to have his way with the Landers bitch, he had been in a morose mood. He had searched the camp for her without success and had eventually concluded that she must be hiding up in the hills. Since then, much joy juice had passed his lips and his wits were addled, but not so much that he couldn't recognize a threat to his authority when he heard one. Staggering to his feet, he grabbed the nearest weapon to hand and rushed for the door. As he flung it open, the first thing he saw in the street was a bearded redcoat astride a massive horse, looking for all the world as though he owned the place.

'*Mon dieu*,' howled the outraged Metis. As he tried to level his heavy 'trapdoor' Springfield, he bellowed down the street at the strangely inactive guards, 'Shoot him down, you fools!' With that he snapped off an ill-judged shot that was far too low.

The heavy bullet slammed into the horse's belly. With warm blood pumping from the lethal wound, the animal screamed in pain and toppled heavily to one side. Unable to jump free in time, Bairstow crashed to the frozen earth with teeth-jarring force. Stunned by the impact, he lay helplessly on the ground with his left leg trapped under the weight of his dying horse.

The sudden outbreak of violence had broken the spell and the three guards jerked into life. Without any answering gunfire, it abruptly occurred to them that the Mountie's dramatic appearance was just a gigantic bluff.

'He's all on his own,' yelled one of the men jubilantly, as he levered up a cartridge in an old Henry Rifle that he had stolen from one of the miners. The other two enthusiastically pointed their weapons down the street. After hours of boredom, the thought of taking pot shots at a largely defenceless foe held great appeal.

Marshal Bronson came around the corner of the wooden building directly behind them, carrying the most effective weapon in the circumstances – his twelve gauge sawn-off.

'One chance only,' he stated flatly. 'Drop your weapons and get on the ground, *now*!'

For the second time that day, the three men froze in shock. It was the guard with the Henry that recovered first and he made the fatal mistake of turning too fast. Outnumbered three to one and with his partner down and possibly injured, Bronson couldn't afford any warning shots. With the stubby weapon supported by his hook, he squeezed the first trigger. There was a loud report and a cloud of black-powder smoke temporarily obscured his victim, but the frenzied screaming testified to the accuracy of the blast. Moving the sawn-off slightly, Bronson discharged the remaining barrel. The second half-breed's thick clothing was no defence and with a strangled cry that man fell back into the Gatling gun, before collapsing to the ground stone dead.

Oblivious to the fact that he was now facing an empty weapon, the last of the three was completely immobilised by sheer terror. As he stood there with eyes like saucers, a stream of urine flowed over his boots. Bronson's lips curled up disdainfully as he slammed the butt of his shotgun into the side of the man's head. That individual collapsed next to his stricken cronies as though he had been pole-axed and lay completely still.

Down the street, Bairstow was in grave trouble. Labeau

had retrieved some more cartridges from the cabin and was now taking aimed shots at the trapped Mountie, who had no option other than to cower behind the vast bulk of his dead horse. He had lost his rifle in the fall and so had drawn his service issue Adams Revolver, but was outgunned by the powerful rifle firing from cover. Every shot seemed to get closer, as the bullets slammed into the blood-soaked belly of the unfortunate animal.

As Kirsty appeared at his side, Bronson moved swiftly behind the Gatling and barked urgently, 'Now's your chance for retribution. That damned redcoat is going to get himself killed if we don't get this cannon spitting lead.'

A long black magazine capable of holding forty cartridges protruded upwards from the top of the multi-barrelled gun. A swift glance told him that it was full. Other magazines were piled near the base of the heavy weapon. Thankfully the Metis had been prepared to repel an attack and that fact would now work in the lawman's favour. Kneeling down, he swivelled the gun on its tripod so that it pointed at Labeau's cabin. Then, taking hold of the hand crank, Bronson glanced up at Kirsty. 'Grip the top of the magazine so that it stays in the hopper, while I show that son of a bitch a thing or two!'

With that, he turned the crank clockwise and all hell broke loose. It was not a single volley, but rather a continuous rapid fire that opened up on Labeau's position. That man had just released the 'trapdoor' to load another cartridge into the breech of his rifle when the first bullet struck the door surround. And then another and another and another! It was not the first time that he had been under fire from such a gun, but it still seemed both incredible and terrifying. The injustice of being shot at with his own rapid-fire weapon was also not lost on him. A steady stream of lead slammed into the rough-cut timber around him, forcing the rebel leader to flee to the rear of the cabin. Even as he ran, a splinter of wood lanced into his left arm and drew a howl of pain from his lips.

Outside, Bairstow had finally dragged himself free from under his dead horse and found that, remarkably, he had no broken bones. Recovering his Winchester, he holstered the Adams and peered down the street at his two companions. The deadly fusillade had abruptly ceased and Bronson bellowed over to him, 'Empty.'

Staggering to his feet, the Mountie ran stiffly to the side and then across the thoroughfare in pursuit of Labeau. There was no wooden sidewalk in such a primitive place, just hard earth or mud, so he hunkered down next to the door. Knowing that there would undoubtedly be a rifle pointing at the entrance, he literally had no idea what to do next.

Bronson, meanwhile, had replaced the empty magazine with a full one. He did have an idea what would happen next. The sheer volume of noise had to have been heard at the diggings. The remaining rebels would most likely assume that the camp was under attack by a posse and that the Gatling was being used to fend it off, which would hopefully give the lawmen an edge.

'We've got no cover here at all,' Bronson muttered to his feisty companion. 'Open the door behind us and we'll drag this tripod back.'

'You just love to give orders, don't you?' she replied, but nevertheless did as she was told.

'I'm a federal officer,' he responded with uncharacteristic pomposity. 'That gives me the right!'

As if adding weight to his words, there came a tremendous pounding of hoofs as Labeau's followers hastened back to the camp.

'Get those other magazines back here fast,' Bronson commanded. 'You had an all-fired hankering for some killing and it looks like you're going to get your wish!'

Kirsty appeared genuinely shocked at such forthright language. There was no hiding the fear in her eyes. She was relatively new to brutal bloody violence and it appeared as though her baptism of fire had only just begun!

CHAPTER EIGHT

Jesse Bronson had the intelligence to realize that, even with the revolutionary rapid firing Gatling, he was still no match for over twenty men if they possessed even an ounce of tactical sense *and* if they were given the chance to use it. He knew that the three of them could only benefit from the 'shock and awe' factor once, so he would have to take full advantage of it. The very fact that the Metis horsemen would inevitably have to bunch up within the confines of the camp's only street would work in the lawman's favour.

'Crouch down behind the gun until I say,' he instructed Kirsty. 'I just hope that damned Canadian has got the sense to get off the street. That crazy red jacket of his acts like a beacon.'

As the drumming hoofs came closer, that very thought occurred to the frontier policeman. It irked him that the Metis leader was unaccounted for, but he knew that he had to get out of sight and fast. Twisting away, he ducked round the corner and then over to the next cabin. With his back up against that, he would be invisible to the horsemen as they came into camp from the same direction that he had. He only just made it!

The massed body of horsemen galloped into Alder Gulch and viciously reined up before Bairstow's dead mount. The apparent lack of activity was not what they had expected and consequently the rebels milled around in confusion. They spied the Gatling gun with three bodies sprawled in front of it, but couldn't immediately make out who they were. Then Labeau's harsh tones boomed out from the rear of the cabin, 'They've got the gun, you morons. Spread out before—' The rest of his words were lost in the mayhem of blood and bullets.

Down the street, Kirsty leapt to her feet to grip the magazine and Bronson pushed forward on the hand crank. He had his hook fixed in a toggle at the back of the gun, which allowed him to easily swivel it from side to side. As a stream of lead spewed out from the multiple barrels, a great cloud of sulphurous smoke gathered in front of the gun, obscuring his view. Not that that really mattered. At such range, the marshal simply couldn't miss.

The heavy bullets scythed into the packed mass of men and horses, puncturing flesh and breaking bone. The rudimentary street rapidly became a place of mud and blood, as the horses churned up the ground and Bronson's shattered victims tumbled on to it. Not even the repeated detonations could blot out the screams of the wounded. The machine gun was remorseless, as it ploughed bloody furrows through the Metis horsemen. And then suddenly the crank turned, but no bullets came. The second magazine was empty. The lawman well knew that what happened next depended on whether Labeau's men had any fight left in them and he was soon to find out.

With bloodcurdling howls two men at the front of the pack, who had miraculously escaped harm, spurred their terrified horses forward.

'Get a new magazine in, fast,' Bronson directed as he drew his Remington single action and cocked the hammer. Kirsty didn't need any urging. Tilting the elongated section of metal, she removed it from the hopper, hurled it to the ground and grabbed another. Even as the marshal lined up on the first horse, that being the larger target, he heard shooting from further down the street and correctly surmised that Bairstow was finally contributing to the fight.

The two fast approaching half-breeds had grown up on the Canadian Plains and were excellent horsemen, but even they could not aim accurately at speed. All their opponent needed to do to survive the encounter was to keep his nerve and he possessed that ability. With calm deliberation, Bronson placed his first bullet into the animal's breast. Its forelegs buckled with the shock. As a great gout of blood spurted forth, it slewed sideways and crashed to the ground. Its rider was thrown forward with great force, whilst the other horseman instinctively pulled away to avoid a collision. The man on the ground was at the very least badly stunned, so Bronson chose to fire up at the second man. Even as the gun bucked in his hand, he knew that he'd got it right.

His bullet must have struck a lung, because the Metis spewed out a mouthful of blood and swayed drunkenly in his saddle. The man's horse, frightened by the shooting and sudden lack of control by his rider, bolted at speed.

'Watch out,' screamed Kirsty, as the first man staggered to his feet and drew a belt gun. He appeared disorientated and confused, but Bronson had neither the time nor inclination to take any prisoners. His revolver discharged again and his opponent went down hard and fast.

*

Bairstow considered himself to be a stalwart individual, but as the Gatling had opened up on the packed horsemen at close range, he was able only to observe the butchery in stunned awe. In his time as a policeman, he had never experienced anything like it before, not even in the final battle with the Metis back in May. It was only when the weapon had ceased firing that he realized he had to get involved, otherwise his two companions were in danger of being overrun whilst reloading.

With his shoulders against the cabin wall, he sighted down the barrel of his Winchester on to a broad back and squeezed the trigger. Then, with practised ease, he levered and fired repeatedly into the rear of the remaining horsemen. More riders tumbled to the ground creating further chaos and confusion. And then, at the other end of the street, Bronson turned the crank again and their victory was complete. No men could endure such slaughter.

As the bullets scythed relentlessly into them, the few surviving Metis despairingly broke and fled. Then, abruptly and well before its time, the Gatling ceased belching forth death. There was a blockage in its intricate mechanism that would take time to clear. The fugitives reined in and weighed up their suddenly unexpected options. They really didn't fancy charging back up that blood-soaked thoroughfare. Then a harsh, heavily accented voice bellowed out from a nearby cabin.

'Kill that cursed Mountie,' demanded Labeau. 'He is surely behind all this.'

As half a dozen enraged Metis turned their horses towards him, Corporal Bairstow ran as though the hounds of hell were after him. He knew that he couldn't outrun horses for long, but he just needed to get to the rear of the cabin.

With the pounding of many hoofs closing on him, he reached the corner and flung himself around it. As a shot rang out, a hastily aimed bullet slammed into nearby timber.

Reluctantly dropping flat on to the cloying mud, Bairstow then slid sideways under the floorboards of the cabin. He was greeted by the overwhelming stink of urine and excrement. Some of the camp's inhabitants obviously hadn't been bothered to trail to the river. Almost retching, he lay there in the semi-darkness covered in slime, listening to the pursuing horsemen rounding the corner. As they milled about in disbelief, he aimed his rifle at the light and waited.

As the cloud of acrid smoke gradually cleared, Bronson glanced down at the pile of brass cartridges around the tripod. He felt sick to his stomach at such carnage. He had signed on as a deputy marshal to improve his own lot and that of his country, not slaughter countless human beings. Shaking his head, he knew that he had to get a grip. Kirsty had already disobeyed him by running off down the street brandishing his Winchester. He knew full well that there could be any number of wounded, but still dangerous, rebels. Grabbing his shotgun, the lawman loaded it on the run – a difficult task with only one hand.

At close quarters, the street resembled a slaughterhouse. Bullets from the Gatling had struck men and horses indiscriminately. Yet whether any of them could actually be saved was something that would have to wait. As renewed firing broke out, Bronson observed a clutch of horsemen at the far end of the street. They were spurring their horses off to the left and could only be chasing one thing: a red tunic.

Bellowing at Kirsty to stand fast, he raced off between the cabins. Reaching the end of the short alleyway, the lawman glanced down the uneven line of buildings. The surviving rebels were clustered around the back of a cabin. From the indentations in the mud, their prey had obviously gone to ground, but none of them showed any inclination to pursue him. After so much slaughter, it would likely only take the threat of more violence to break their shaky resolve and so Bronson tucked the shotgun into his shoulder and took aim. The stubby barrels rested on his left forearm and after a short hesitation he raised them slightly before squeezing one trigger. There had been enough killing for one day!

The lethal shot discharged harmlessly into the air above the riders, but it was enough to make them turn tail and run. The skulking Mountie had suddenly become irrelevant and they were all too well aware that their dead greatly outnumbered the survivors.

Replacing the smoking cartridge, Bronson cautiously approached Bairstow's bolthole. 'It's safe to come out now,' he remarked drily.

There came a muffled obscenity, followed by a deal of scuffling before the mud-soaked Canadian finally emerged. Despite the circumstances, it was impossible for the Montana marshal to repress a smile. 'Looks like you Mounties have finally learned the benefit of camouflage,' he drolly remarked. Before the other man could reply, he turned and guardedly headed over to the main street. He was concerned about Kirsty and the lack of gunfire did nothing to allay his fears.

Bronson found her standing in a daze, amidst a scene of pure carnage. His Winchester had slipped from her grasp, as she vainly struggled to come to terms with the shocking spectacle. Other than the young woman, every creature in sight, either two or four legged, was washed with blood.

Cries of anguish emanated from those rebels who were wounded and helpless. They pleaded for their comrades to assist them, but their entreaties went unanswered. Labeau and his remaining men had apparently made good their escape, if in fact that was what they had done.

Suddenly, as the lawman moved over to join her, fresh movement registered on his peripheral vision. More people were approaching on foot from the direction of the diggings and he instinctively shifted his shotgun to cover them.

'Hold on, Marshal,' Kirsty intoned swiftly. The possibility of more violence had brought her to her senses. 'They're my people.'

As Deckard Foster led the residents of Alder Gulch back into their camp, he could not possibly have been prepared for the scene that would greet him. The blood-soaked street, covered by dead or wounded men and animals, provided a gruesome backdrop for the only man left standing. He was a tall, heavily built individual with a drooping moustache. There was an unquestionable air of authority about him that was not only attributable to the lethal twelve gauge in his grasp. Then his glance took in Kirsty's familiar form and with relief he realized that the newcomer had to have returned with her.

'Easy with that shotgun, mister,' implored Foster, holding his hands out palm first. 'We're nothing to do with those murdering sons of bitches.'

If he had expected a response, he was to be disappointed. The somewhat menacing individual gazed at him blankly without lowering the gun, as though deep in thought. In spite of his impressive size and position as the camp's enforcer, Foster felt strangely uneasy as he regarded the lone gunman. With unaccustomed nervousness, he tried again.

'Are you some kind of lawman? Only we were in real need of help up here.'

Finally his entreaties seemed to register. With a sigh, the big man carefully lowered his weapon and then opened his shaggy coat. Pinned to his chest was the worn badge that they had so hoped to see.

'The name's Bronson. Deputy US marshal out of Billings. The howdy do's will have to wait.' His tone was brisk and no nonsense, as though he had just thought everything through and now required instant co-operation. 'I need to know just where those sons of bitches have gone and what their intentions might be, so get some men up into the hills to check around. Then I need some of you to disarm the wounded. Anyone not dead could still be dangerous. Oh, and get that Gatling off the street.'

Foster blinked uncertainly as he absorbed the blizzard of instructions. He wasn't used to being spoken to in such an abrupt manner and it didn't sit well. 'Now hold on, Marshal. My name's Deckard Foster. I run the vigilance committee for the camp.' Then, as though sensing that that wasn't quite enough, he added, 'Kirsty'll vouch for me.'

Bronson regarded the large hairy individual with some impatience. An icy smile spread across his features, as he pointedly glanced around at the carnage. 'Well, *Deckard Foster*, it's plain for all to see that you haven't been all that vigilant. In case you hadn't noticed, you've been a prisoner in your own camp! Now I'm the duly appointed federal authority in these parts and if we're going to make this senseless slaughter count for anything at all, then you're going to have to do as I say. Savvy?' The other man nodded silently. It was clear that he hadn't yet adjusted to the change in circumstances, but the lawman wasn't finished. 'Never complain and never explain. That little motto's served me well enough over the years, but this once I'm going to make an exception. The reason I want that Gatling off the street and out of action is because otherwise we'll waste time guarding something that has no good purpose anymore. Now that you and your *vigilantes* have got your guns back, Labeau hasn't got the men left to storm this place again and such a cumbersome weapon is useless out there in the hills. So it makes more sense to strip it down and hide it than give them the chance to steal it back. One last thing to think on. There's snow in the air and those Canadians are well used to harsh winters. If we're not careful we could find ourselves cut off and under siege.'

Foster didn't care to be referred to as a vigilante, but he let it pass. Besides, he suddenly had something else to think about. A tall individual, coated in mud and brandishing a rifle, had just emerged from the nearest alley. Bronson caught the movement in his peripheral vision and the ghost of a smile crossed his hard features.

'This here's a *dis*mounted policeman from north of the border. He prefers crawling to riding.'

That was too much for the aggrieved Mountie. 'Now just a God damned minute, Bronson!'

The big marshal guffawed and shook his head. 'Just funning, Corporal. Just funning.' It was obvious to him that Foster had something to say and the lawman was keenly aware that, standing around in the street, they were all mightily vulnerable.

The camp's enforcer had decided that Deputy Bronson clearly knew what he was about, but he was puzzled. 'Why would those curs concern themselves with us anymore?

They're more than likely headed north on the river by now. When I send some men out, we'll know for sure.'

The lawman was completely nonplussed. 'The river! How do you figure that out?'

It was Foster's turn to appear confused. He turned to Kirsty and put the question, 'Didn't you tell him about the rafts?'

The young lady casually shrugged, but nonetheless coloured with embarrassment. 'I didn't think it was important. How could I know that the three of us would put them all to flight?'

Bronson fumed with exasperation. 'Girl, because of you I could have left the back door open. So from now on you let me decide just what's important. Savvy?'

Conscious of many eyes on her, she nodded silently.

Switching back to the enforcer, the marshal demanded, 'So talk to me. What have those half-breeds been up to?'

Foster took the time to instruct some of his men to scout around, before answering that question. 'That Labeau is no fool, but he is also very lucky. He and his scum just happened to turn up here when the camp had three years' worth of mined gold stockpiled. Because we are so remote and there's no railhead anywhere close, it made sense to hold on to it . . . until now. It means that bastard has stolen everything that we possess.' The big man's voice cracked slightly as he related the sorry tale. 'Anyway, he knew that with winter coming on, he might struggle to get the gold out of here if the camp got snowed in.' Foster glanced curiously at the bedraggled Mountie. 'He thought that someone might be after him, so he set his men to building rafts. The river flows into the Missouri and that's navigable all the way down to Great Falls. That's where it all stops, because there are five waterfalls over a ten-mile stretch. Eighty years ago Lewis and Clark portaged past them, but with the load Labeau's carrying that's out of the question. *But*, steamboats come up the river as far as the town. With money and guns, he would have no trouble taking over one of those and then it's on to the Bear Paw Mountains. From there the Canadian border is just spitting distance away.'

Bronson glared angrily at the Mountie. 'Why didn't you think of this? You're supposed to know how your people reason.'

That was entirely too much for the corporal. Striding forward, he placed himself nose to nose with the American. 'They're not *my* people. They are disaffected rebels who don't want anything to do with the new country that we're building. And just how was I to know that we were near the Missouri River? I don't even know where we are. That's why you were ordered out here by Marshal Kelley, *Deputy.*'

Both men's hackles were rising. They could easily have come to blows, had not the return of Foster's men diverted them.

'There's two rafts missing alright, Deckard. They've just taken the ones with crates of gold loaded on. Even so, they're going to be short-handed when they hit rough water with that much weight on board.'

Such a report concentrated everyone's thoughts. The two lawmen both consciously took a deep breath and backed off. The Mountie in particular seemed to have something on his mind. 'Years ago, French voyageurs explored this continent by river, trading and hunting. It's in their blood. If anyone can control heavily laden rafts, Labeau's men can.'

'Oh, great,' fumed Bronson. 'So now we're up against pirates.' His confrontation with Bairstow completely forgotten, he turned away and began to prowl aimlessly around the thoroughfare, deep in thought. Even the moans of the wounded failed to distract him. He knew that, however many opinions might be forthcoming, it was effectively up to him to decide on the next course of action. In reality, he had little choice. Although the bulk of Labeau's men were accounted for and the Gatling recovered, the man himself was still at large. Since Bronson was tasked with apprehending him, it looked like he was about to join the navy.

Returning to the others, he looked pointedly at the Mountie. 'So if you're Canadian, it must mean that you can handle a raft as well.'

Bairstow snorted. 'I'm from English Protestant stock. My forebears were American colonists, loyal to the crown, who escaped up to Canada after the War of Independence. I've never crewed a river raft in my life and don't try to connect me to the scum that we're chasing. But,' he allowed, 'I am prepared to give it a try if you are.'

Kirsty could no longer remain silent. 'Now just you fellows hold on. You're not going anywhere until one of you gets a bullet out of my pa. We were expecting you to bring a sawbones along and you haven't, so now it's up to you.' Fixing her fiery gaze on Bronson, she added, 'You've obviously shot plenty in your time, so it stands to reason that you know how to pull the lead out again. And as a federal officer it's your sworn duty to help!'

The marshal had the sense to know when he was stonewalled and he couldn't deny that she had the right of it. It also made more sense to set off in the morning, once the raft had been appraised and provisioned.

Foster added his own contribution. 'Those thieving bastards will be mighty low in the water with all that weight. It'll slow them down plenty. *And* they'll likely tie up someplace come dark, because they don't know the river any better than you do.'

'All right, all right, you've convinced me,' conceded Bronson. 'I'll need liquor, towels, a thin blade and a fire to heat it in. Show me where the patient is!'

Two things occurred that evening that were likely to have grave consequences for all the various occupants of Alder Gulch. It began to snow hard and Kirsty's father finally died, under the knife. The heavy snowfall did at least mean that the fresh cadavers would stay that way; free from corruption and foul odours until the miners had chance to dispose of them. The latter occurrence was entirely free of any redeeming features.

Already drifting in and out of consciousness, Kirk Landers had been heavily dosed with laudanum. In his time, Marshal Bronson had witnessed the extraction of many bullets and intended to draw on that experience. Unfortunately, he had barely begun to probe the infected wound when the poor man gave a tremendous shudder, emitted a muted groan and suddenly lay very still. It was decided that most likely his heart had given out. In a way it was a blessing, because at least his suffering was over, but his daughter could hardly be expected to view it that way.

Sometime after this traumatic event, Kirsty and the two lawmen were standing in the large cabin at the end of the street, which the Metis had used as a meeting house. It had been turned into a makeshift operating room, although with the demise of Kirk Landers there were no longer any patients left. Deckard Foster and some of the more blood-thirsty miners had gone out in the encroaching darkness and finished off the wounded marauders. With their cries for mercy ignored, muzzle flashes flared eerily in the night, as gunshots echoed around the ravine.

Bronson and Bairstow exchanged meaningful glances, but made no move to stop the premeditated slaughter. They well knew that the isolated settlement did not have the facilities to house and treat wounded prisoners and both men understood that the miners were out to avenge weeks of fear and oppression. The death of their comrade had been the last straw. The main priority for the lawmen was now to get some much-needed sleep, but Kirsty wasn't quite ready to let them rest. Since the death of her father she had been understandably silent and morose, but that was about to change.

'I'm going with you on the raft,' she announced. 'I want to be there when you catch up with Labeau.'

Bronson had been expecting some such nonsense and was ready for her. 'Now wait just a God damned minute, young lady. This isn't going to be a joy ride and we're not taking passengers, period!' He looked to the Mountie for support, but that man was strangely silent.

Conscious of a possible ally, Kirsty tried a new tack. 'Do either of you know this river? Have either of you ever handled a raft before? Because believe me they can be as ornery as a mule and twice as dangerous.'

Before the marshal could offer a retort, Bairstow finally spoke and there was no hiding the interest in his eyes as he viewed her closely. 'How would you know rafts or the river? You're a miner's daughter, not a voyageur.'

Despite her grief, Kirsty couldn't hide a triumphant smile as she replied. 'My pa and some others rafted down to Great Falls for supplies in the summer and then came back overland. They took me with them, so I know where the white water is and a good place where Labeau could fort up and take you – *us* by surprise. So you see you really do need me.'

The Mountie gazed at her with frank admiration and maybe something else in his eyes. His unprofessional interest was not missed by the marshal, but that man was just too tired for another confrontation. He held his arms up in mock surrender and turned away, but still managed to have the last word by supplying a chilling reminder of what they were up against. 'This isn't just a lark, you know, Kirsty. If it all goes wrong, you won't even end up in a cold hole in the ground with your pa. You'll be feeding the fishes at the bottom of the Missouri River!'

CHAPTER NINE

Jesse Bronson took his first look at the raft and didn't like what he saw. He didn't like it one little bit. His disquiet must have showed plainly, because Bairstow edged up next to him and put an obvious question. 'Can you swim, Bronson?'

The marshal glared fiercely at him. 'What do you think I am, some damn fool kid? Of course I can swim.'

With that he stalked over to the rudimentary landing beyond the camp and clambered gingerly on to the waiting conveyance. As it wallowed slightly under his weight, his eyes widened like saucers. Although the raft was securely tied to two solid posts sunk into the riverbank, the water was flowing past at speed and left nothing to the imagination. His sense of balance was also affected by something else. The snow had ceased to fall hours before, but the untrimmed logs that made up the structure had a good coating that was only then turning to slush.

Conscious of the Mountie's eyes still on him, Bronson made great play of examining the craft that was to carry them downriver in pursuit of the fugitives. It was easily twenty feet in length and probably two thirds of that in width. The front end was V shaped, presumably to aid their progress through the water, and the marshal had to admit that the whole thing appeared to be solidly put together. But then of course it had been intended to carry very heavy crates of stolen gold. Did that mean that without such a cargo, they would be dangerously unstable?

As his eyes feverishly roved about, they took in the small shelter situated amidships. It was made of rough boards and could accommodate the three of them at a push, if they all huddled together. On his instructions, the Gatling gun, covered by a tarpaulin, had been roped and pegged to the logs just in front of the shelter. A single steering oar was located at the rear of the vessel. He shuddered at the thought of attempting to control that in rough weather. 'What if I fall overboard, for Christ's sake?' he pondered.

As though uncannily reading his thoughts, Deckard Foster had some advice for the visibly shaken marshal. 'Water is very fickle. You have to watch it all the time, especially now, after all the rain that there's been up in the hills. The river's running fast and deep.'

Bronson gazed over at the camp's enforcer. The burly individual had arrived to watch their departure and was stood at the water's edge, observing him closely. To the marshal's heightened imagination, it seemed as though everyone was scrutinizing him that morning.

'And I'd advise you to listen to Kirsty,' the miner added. 'She may be only young, but she has made this journey before. She's sharp and plucky and can tell you what to look out for.'

It was at that moment that the young lady herself appeared, followed by one of the miners carrying provisions for the raft. She was heavily muffled up and obviously well prepared for conditions on the river. Her eyes were red-rimmed from crying over her father as he was laid to rest in a hastily excavated grave, but there was no doubting her determination. 'Ready when you are, gentlemen,' she forthrightly announced to her two travelling companions.

Before the Mountie was able to respond, Bronson snapped back, 'I'll do the telling!' With that he promptly turned away and hurried off towards the nearest stand of timber. 'But first I've got something to attend to,' he bawled out by way of explanation.

'Easy to see he's no sailor,' Bairstow remarked drily. 'First sign of deep water and he needs to take a shit!'

Luke Tasker twitched nervously at the sight of the four horsemen heading towards him through the snow-covered trees. He had not expected to encounter anyone so far from the camp. Having watched the departure of Kirsty and the two lawmen on the lone raft, the young miner had decided to enjoy his recently regained freedom by going hunting. Meat stocks in the settlement were low, after weeks of occupation by the marauders.

With their faces muffled against the cold, Luke had no idea who the men were, but something about them worried him. No one had any good reason to be out in the foothills of the Rockies in winter. He briefly considered hightailing it, but the conditions were not ideal for speed and besides, he had a stubborn streak. Unlike most of the miners, the young man was not completely unfamiliar with gunplay. He had spent a year as a deputy town marshal in Rapid City, Dakota Territory before coming to his senses and getting a less challenging job. Dismounting, he placed himself so that his horse shielded him from the strangers. Sliding the barrel of his Winchester over the saddle, Luke levered in a brass cartridge.

'I reckon that's far enough, gents,' he called out firmly. 'Let's have a palaver before you get any closer.'

As the four men reined in about twenty-five yards away, Luke got his first good look at them and fear began to gnaw at his guts. All of their features continued to remain hidden, with only their eyes uncovered *and* one of them was absolutely enormous. That veritable bear of a man turned to glance at his cronies and nodded. As if by pre-arrangement, they all began to spread out in a semi-circle around the young miner. Despite the cold, moist atmosphere, Luke's mouth was suddenly bone dry. Gesturing with his rifle, he managed to cry out, 'Don't move or I'll fire!'

'*Don't,*' echoed the giant. 'Who tells me, "don't"?'

All the time the menacing riders continued their approach, so Luke drew a bead on the largest – and quite obviously most dangerous – of them. But then he hesitated, because it's a hell of a thing to kill a fellow human being without good cause. The man before him had no such scruples. He abruptly aimed some kind of massive horse-pistol and fired.

The large ball slammed into soft flesh and Luke's mount staggered under the blow, emitting a high-pitched scream of agony. Before the young man could leap clear, it collapsed on its side, pinning both of his legs. As he in turn fell back into the snow, his finger convulsed on the trigger, sending a bullet whining off harmlessly into the trees. He cried out in pain under the crushing weight, but somehow instinctively realized that he still had to defend himself.

Levering in another cartridge, he raised up over the quivering body of his horse. Luke's eyes had filled with tears, which affected his vision, and it was only with great difficulty that he located a target. The rifle's foresight briefly settled on a torso and he squeezed the trigger. As his shoulder absorbed the recoil, he uttered a great moan and collapsed back to the ground. The agony from his damaged legs was overwhelming and it was about all he could do to remain conscious.

Dutch Henry Bruckner dropped down from his horse and lumbered over to his prone victim. Off to his left a man known as Black Bart was howling in pain and surprise as blood flowed from a shoulder wound. He and the other gun thug had been recruited in White Sulphur Springs. Cocking his Colt Dragoon, the huge man aimed it directly at Luke's face and was about to fire when there came that word again.

'*Don't* kill him, Dutch! We need him alive.'

That man snorted derisively, but nevertheless held his fire. Instead he effortlessly wrenched the Winchester out of Luke's hands and placed a huge boot proprietorially on his chest. Only then did he turn to view the individual who had dared to interrupt a killing.

'I don't take to that God damned word, you maggot. My pa used it every time he beat on me, until he did it once too often.'

Nelson Pruitt pulled the scarf away from his face, before holding up his hands in a placatory gesture. 'I didn't mean nothing by it, Dutch. Only if he's from Alder Gulch, he's either escaped or something grievous has happened down there. Either way it wouldn't hurt to parley with him awhile.'

The big man favoured him with a mirthless smile. 'Fair enough. But because you've mentioned my name *twice*, he's going to have to die anyway. Whether he goes hard or easy depends on how helpful he is.' At that, he turned to see what effect his words had had on the young man.

Luke was in too much pain to fully comprehend his dire

situation, but the sudden sight of Nelson Pruitt looming over him brought a strangled cry from his lips. 'You!'

'That's right, sonny,' replied that man. 'Thought I'd come back and see how my *amigos* in Alder Gulch were getting along and it seems to me you don't look so good.'

Furious anger flooded through Luke's veins. It had been bad enough being occupied by foreign rebels, but Pruitt was a fellow American who had spent some time in the camp with Labeau before disappearing. 'You bastard,' he yelled. 'Why can't you just leave us alone?'

Pruitt sniggered. 'That's not very friendly. All we wanted was a short parley and yet you've put a bullet in my friend.' From behind them and as though to emphasize the injustice of it all, Bart groaned in anguish as the fourth man examined the wound. 'Anyhow, what news from the camp?' continued the outlaw with a show of fake bonhomie. 'Have you given Labeau's men the slip?'

Luke was too far down the tortuous spiral of pain to play word games. He just wanted relief from his torment. 'Alder Gulch is free of those scum,' he spat out. 'Most of them are dead, killed by a US marshal. Name of Bronson.'

Bruckner and Pruitt exchanged startled glances. 'And what of their leader?' the latter demanded. 'And all the gold that he seized?'

That was the cruncher and if Luke had had his wits about him, he could have used his knowledge as a bargaining tool, but the crushing weight of the dead horse was bearing down terribly on his injured legs. 'Labeau's on the river heading for the Bear Paw Mountains . . . on two rafts with the gold . . . Bronson's gone after them with the Gatling gun . . . the girl too.'

The two outlaws drew together as though Luke no longer

existed. 'What girl?' queried Dutch Henry.

'How the hell should I know,' responded Pruitt petulantly. 'What's it matter? It's the gold that I – we want and at least we know where it's going.'

'How's that help us?' the big man retorted. 'We can't overhaul them on horseback.'

'We don't need to chase them,' the other man replied soothingly. He well knew that it was dangerous to antagonize his brutish companion. 'We just need to be around to pick up the pieces, after that bastard marshal has finished with him. And don't forget, crates of gold are mighty heavy. There won't be any portaging. Labeau will come to a dead stop at Great Falls, at least until he can muster up some more transport. That's where we'll probably catch him. What happens then depends on how many men he's got left. We can either kill him or join him. *But*, however you judge such things, we're likely to come into a nice piece of change!'

As he mulled over the changed situation, Dutch Henry stared long and hard at the remaining Pruitt brother. The big man did not possess a keen intelligence, but he was not stupid by any means. He realized that Nelson had been right not to immediately kill the young hunter, but that that individual's usefulness was now played out. With a contented grunt, he slowly drew his skinning knife from its sheath and bent down over his jaw-droppingly terrified prisoner.

'You've done told us all we need to know, boy. And since I don't feel inclined to waste powder and ball on you, it looks like I'll just have to get to whittling.'

Nelson Pruitt regarded Dutch Henry with revulsion and quickly turned away. Killing in cold blood had never bothered him, but that huge maniac took a sick pleasure in his work that made Pruitt wish he hadn't eaten so many beans the night before. As he made his way over to the other two men, hideous screams began to reverberate around the hillside.

'Sweet Jesus,' lamented Jesse Bronson unhappily. 'No amount of gold is worth all this.'

Since leaving the landing stage at Alder Gulch, the lawman had been in a world of hurt. He was out of his element and he knew it, but that did not improve matters. To his jaundiced mind, the raft seemed to be ungovernable as it sped along on a strong current. The water eddied and whirled, creating an ever-present background noise that did nothing to calm his rattled nerves. They appeared to glide past the riverbanks with the pace of a steam locomotive, but such rapid progress provided little solace to the unhappy passenger. Bronson was squatting uncomfortably between the rudimentary shelter and the Gatling gun. He had his iron hook desperately wedged in a toggle at the rear of the gun, in an attempt to keep his balance. His trousers' legs were soaked with spray and he felt an urge to be sick.

Kirsty, in an attempt to take her mind off her father's demise, had effectively assumed the role of captain. She had recruited the Mountie to assist her on the sweep at the rear of the craft. Requiring, as it did, close proximity, he had jumped at the chance and was enthusiastically following her instructions.

'At this speed we'll soon catch up with those murdering varmints,' she called out stridently.

'Be careful what you wish for,' returned Bronson sourly. 'This ain't the best place for a fire fight.'

And the marshal had good reason for such a comment,

because conditions on board the raft were not the only things preying on his mind. For instance, why had Labeau not cut loose the remaining vessels? It was almost as though the rebel leader was daring the lawmen to follow him. Although he was unlikely to have prior knowledge of the Missouri River, he was in the lead and would be quite able to spot a good place for an ambush.

Nodding to himself as though his mind was made up, Bronson bellowed out to the two figures at the stern. 'I know you seem to be enjoying this boat trip, but I think we're heading into a trap. You say you rode this river in the summer?'

'That I did,' Kirsty briskly responded.

'Right then. I need to know when we approach a pinch point. Narrows in the river, with cliffs overlooking it or some such. Do you understand me, girl?'

The young woman surrendered the steering oar to the Mountie and edged closer to her inquisitor. The raft lurched as Bairstow adjusted his grip on the long pole, but she barely seemed to notice.

'Don't treat me like some snotty child, Marshal Bronson! I know exactly what you mean and there just happens to be such a place. You'll get fair warning of our approach. Just make sure you don't fall overboard before we get there.' She paused and then just couldn't resist adding, 'Mind you, there's no need to worry. You'd likely be knocked senseless on a rock before you had chance to drown painfully.'

Samuel Bairstow laughed out loud at the horrified expression on his companion's grizzled features. 'That young woman sure has spunk,' he decided before following up with a comment of his own. 'Well they do say that there is always worse trouble at sea.'

*

It was only due to the fact that Jacques Labeau was finally getting used to the motion of the raft that he was able to concentrate on his dark and devious schemes. His forebears might have been voyageurs, but he felt far happier on a horse. Events had taken a dreadful turn in Alder Gulch for sure, but that didn't mean the game was up. He still possessed enough gold to equip an army. *If* he could turn it into cash money *and* spend it in the right places before getting killed or seized by that God damned Mountie. It was for that reason that he had taken the apparently strange decision to leave the remaining rafts tied up at the landing stage. It was better to know exactly where his enemies were than to have them roaming around like loose cannons.

It was as the light began to drain out of the sky that he saw exactly what he wanted. A cliff of granite projected out into the Missouri, narrowing it considerably and obscuring the stretch of river beyond. The water was already flowing faster, leaving him little time to react. Bellowing over to the leading raft, he instructed, 'Marcel, pull into the bank once we've rounded the headland.'

That individual offered a brief wave of acknowledgement and began to heave on the sweep. He had three men on his raft, whilst Labeau only had two. Seven men in total: all that remained from the large band that the rebel leader had led south of the border earlier in the year. Labeau knew that the massive reverse at the Montana mining camp had badly affected his credibility as a leader. It would not be easy getting Marcel to agree to his next plan.

The two heavily-laden rafts passed dangerously close to the cliff and then swung sharply as they headed towards the riverbank. On each craft a man crouched ready with a rope, watching for a tree or heavy rock to use as a land anchor. As the lead vessel came close, the oarsman heaved on the sweep causing the stern to swing over. The crates of gold creaked alarmingly as they strained against the thick rope that secured them to the timber. A nimble Metis leaped across the narrowing gap and swiftly ran a line around the nearest tree. As he took the strain, the rope went taut. They had made it.

The second raft drifted in and the procedure was repeated so that within minutes both vessels were securely tied up. Labeau ordered that additional lines be used. He wasn't taking any chances with such a cargo. Knowing that any pursuers were unlikely to arrive before morning, he then allowed a small cooking fire to be lit. He needed his men to be well fed and compliant, particularly those who were to bear the brunt of his scheme. Most especially it was Marcel who needed to be convinced, because he was to spring the trap!

'I have a small task for you, *mon chéri*,' Labeau announced in a soft and soothing voice. He sounded as though he had just given his companion a present, but then came the sting in the tail. 'You may not welcome it, but it is necessary.'

The other man regarded his leader suspiciously. They had eaten well on meat and beans taken from the camp and were now sat out of earshot of the others. It was rare indeed for Jacques Labeau to display any great warmth to his subordinates. He preferred to rule by a combination of fear and success, but the latter had been in short supply of late.

'That red-coated policeman and his Yankee marshal are following us. I can smell them. Come the new day, I want you and the crew of your raft to remain here and kill them.

Under your guns, exposed on those narrows, they will stand no chance.'

Marcel's eyes registered a mixture of surprise and discomfort. 'But why, Jacques? What is there to gain by splitting your force when we are now so very few?'

Labeau regarded him closely. Had that last question also contained a criticism? He could feel himself tensing as he always did before the onset of violence, but he knew that he had to control his vicious temper. He needed the assistance of this underling. Patiently, he explained his reasoning.

'We no longer have the American, Nelson Pruitt, to broker the sale of the gold. I need to find people to either buy it or exchange it for weapons. When we reach Great Falls, we'll need a steamer to take us on to the Bear Paw Mountains and we might have to wait awhile. Even then we will still have many miles to travel overland before reaching the Canadian border. We will need to buy or steal wagons to move the crates. We can't do all that with those law dogs on our backs. Once you have killed them, you can follow on and re-join us.'

Marcel's indecision was pitiful to see and Labeau had to curb his impatience.

'But Jacques, if we return to Saskatchewan we'll be hunted down by those cursed redcoats.'

'It's winter,' the Metis leader responded. 'If this Bairstow and his marshal friend are dead, then no one in Ottawa will even know that we have returned. We can head west and plan another uprising. So enough of this. Just do as I ask and all will be well.'

Labeau didn't think to mention what he had already considered. That if by some miracle one of the lawmen survived and took possession of the gold on the raft, then that man would have no choice other than to carry on downstream with the current, straight into the arms of the remaining Metis. Either way the few survivors would be able to return home undetected and as considerably richer men, because in truth the rebel leader had tired of following a lost cause. With their chief, Louis Riel, either hanged or in prison, the rebellion was over for good, so there was no harm in his followers looking after themselves.

CHAPTER TEN

'That place you wanted to know about, with narrows and a cliff overlooking the river,' Kirsty called from the bow. 'We'll be there soon.'

Bronson scrambled unsteadily to his feet, He had been languishing miserably in the shelter, leaving the two younger people to man the raft. It had taken all his will power just to get back on it after spending the hours of darkness on solid ground. His stomach felt queasy and he loathed the motion of the ungainly craft, but all that was suddenly forgotten.

'How far?' he barked out.

The young woman looked mildly apologetic. 'It's hard to tell. Maybe a mile or so. I've only been here the once.'

'Pull into the bank,' commanded the suddenly rejuvenated marshal.

The Mountie looked startled. 'Just what are you about?'

'Just pull in, God damn it all to hell!'

With Kirsty assisting on the sweep, the raft headed in towards the tree-lined riverbank. As the gap narrowed, Bronson jumped eagerly ashore and even with only one hand soon made fast to the nearest tree. The plan that had been simmering in his mind could now come to the boil.

'If my hunch is correct, those poxy sons of bitches are aiming to parole us all to Jesus by way of an ambuscade. *But,* we're going to get the drop on them instead. You're going to wait here, while I make my way down the bank.'

'Wouldn't you rather stay on the raft, Deputy?' Bairstow interrupted. 'And maybe let me do the walking.'

'Go to hell in a handcart,' Bronson responded, with the first sign of a smile for over twenty-four hours. 'You give me some time to get situated and then cast off. They're going to be expecting at least two men, so we're going to need to bulk you up a bit, little lady.' So saying, he removed his heavy coat and handed it over. 'You're going to have to handle the Gatling, while she steers, Samuel.'

The Mountie blinked in surprise. 'That's the first time you've called me by my given name. I didn't even think you'd remembered it.'

The marshal guffawed. 'I must be getting used to having you around. Now listen. When you get within range, empty a magazine at where you think they'll likely be hiding. I'll wait on their reaction and then take them from behind. This scattergun should get their measure.'

Bairstow viewed him with genuine admiration. 'You've really thought this through, haven't you?'

'It took my mind off the gut ache. Anyhow, good luck to you both. And remember, if it all turns out to be a waste of time, then time's all we've lost. We'll still be alive!' With that, he checked both cartridges in his shotgun and then moved off through the trees.

Marcel viewed the raft's departure with mixed feelings. Although he both feared and disliked Jacques Labeau, there was no denying that the rebel leader was a tenacious fighter.

Yet an independent command was now his, so he had better make the best of it, for all their sakes.

The four men were standing on the rear slope of the granite cliff. Although steep, it was easily accessible from the riverbank. With armed and capable men on top of it, even facing the Missouri River's fast flowing current, it would be an easy task to pick off the occupants of any approaching craft – sufficiently easy to spare one of the men for other duties. Marcel had no doubt that the pursuing lawmen were tough, experienced men. They had to have been to retake the camp so easily, so it made good sense to guard the back door. Accordingly, he detailed one of the Metis to move off into the trees near the base of the slope. That man settled down on his haunches, rifle at the ready and alert to any movement.

The other three clambered on up to the top, carefully avoiding the slippery remnants of the snow. Lowering himself carefully on to the smooth, hard surface, Marcel peered over the edge. There was a sheer drop down to where the deep, icy torrent slammed into the rock, which meant that they were unassailable from the front. A surge of enthusiasm suddenly swept through him. If they kept out of sight, surprise would be total and the lawmen really wouldn't stand a chance.

'How long should we give him?' queried Kirsty, with every show of genuine anxiety.

Samuel Bairstow had no easy answer to that. 'That kind of depends on just how far away we actually are, and how long it takes that old man to get there. Not to mention what he intends doing once he is.' He gazed on her careworn, but still very attractive features. 'You're worried about him, aren't you?'

She twitched with surprise. 'Yes, yes I suppose I am. He sort of grows on you after a while, doesn't he?'

'Yeah, like a case of the clap,' replied the Mountie with mock severity. Then in a more considered response, 'Yes, I suppose he does, and yet only a few days ago we were trying to kill each other. How stupid does that seem now?' He shook his head, as though trying to make sense of it all. 'Oh hell, we've been here long enough. Let's get on down that river.' So saying, he carefully loosened the tarpaulin from around the Gatling and reached for one of the long black magazines. 'Can you manage the sweep by yourself?'

'It's no different to riding a horse,' Kirsty replied very implausibly as she jumped lithely ashore to untie the rope. 'So don't you worry about me, Mr Policeman. They breed women tough down here in Montana.'

He didn't doubt it for one minute and that fact somehow only reinforced his desire to see an awful lot more of Kirsty Landers.

Bronson moved carefully through the trees, his shotgun held at the ready but not cocked. If he were to trip over a root and 'pop a cap', the outcome could be grave in all senses of the word. The fast flowing river was some fifty yards off to his right and it wasn't long before he was silently cursing the Metis, Bairstow and Kirsty Landers. His surge of relief at getting clear of that damned raft was now dampened by the hard going on land. Every footfall had to be scrutinized, even as he searched for signs of life to his front. Then, at last, he saw it.

Suddenly lit by a burst of winter sunlight, the gleaming cliff was just visible through the dense trees. The lawman's dark thoughts dissipated, as he realized that the young lady had actually got it right on the nose. Now all he needed was for the precipice to be occupied. Tucking the sawn-off under his left arm, he drew out the indispensable field glasses and cautiously closed the gap.

It was as he moved nearer that he saw the carelessly handled rifle barrel jut out over the side of the crest. Oh, there was someone up there all right. The question was, had they had the sense to guard their rear? Rapidly squatting down in a mixture of leaves and slush, he used his glasses to minutely examine the ground around the reverse of the cliff. The sludge had various boot prints in it, but that was only to be expected. What he was really searching for were prints moving away from that position. It took him only a moment to spot them.

'Stop moving about,' Marcel hissed angrily. 'If you give us away, I'll shoot you myself!'

The target of his rebuke cursed quietly, but stopped wriggling. The melting snow had soaked into their clothes as they lay on the rock and they were all freezing, but there was nothing to be done. They had to wait on the arrival of their pursuers for as long as it took.

Marcel ceased glowering at his subordinate and raised his head for a quick glance at the long stretch of river. What he saw brought a surge of excitement through his body and a slight tightness to his chest. Moving towards their position at speed was a raft with two people on board. One manned the sweep, whilst the other knelt in front of the shelter, near some kind of covering. The cursed Yankees had arrived, just as Labeau had surmised!

*

'You see anything, Bairstow?'

'Yeah, a big lump of rock,' responded that man, all the time wishing that she would address him by his first name. 'But then that's what we're expected to see, so here goes!'

Swiftly removing the tarpaulin, the lawman fixed a magazine into place. With forty rounds ready to descend into the hopper, he seized hold of the crank and elevated the six-barrelled monster as best he could. One man alone couldn't hope to maintain a steady fire for long with such a weapon, especially as its firing base was never still. All he could hope to do was scare the bejesus out of whoever was up there.

With the cliff looming towards them at a frightening pace, the Mountie drew in a deep breath and pushed forward on the crank. The central shaft around which the barrels were grouped began to rotate and immediately stone chips flew off near the summit. The raft's exhilarating speed prevented him from being shrouded by the usual fog of war. All sense of danger was forgotten as he revelled in the sheer power of the amazing weapon.

Marcel and his three companions were just about to rise up and fire on the Americans, when the first bullet struck their outcrop. After that, a seemingly unending stream of lead peppered the cliff face. 'It's that cursed Gatling again,' he cried out in impotent rage. Having been so brutally used in Alder Gulch, the Metis knew that they could do nothing until the magazine was expended. 'As soon as he stops firing, gun them down like the dogs that they are!'

Even though he had expected it, the rapid gunfire made Bronson's heart leap. It took a conscious effort to remain silently in place. The hidden gunman that he sought reacted less well. About ten yards away, foliage shifted as that individual desperately attempted to discover what was happening. The seasoned lawman knew what needed to be done. There was simply no time to pussyfoot about. Cocking both hammers of the sawn-off, he took rapid aim and discharged both barrels at the hidden gun thug. The recoil was punishing, but the big gun did its job. At such range the spread of shot was lethal. With his gamble rewarded by agonized screaming, Bronson swiftly shifted position and reloaded the twelve gauge. He had a feeling that the bloodletting had only just begun.

Muffled up in Bronson's huge coat, Kirsty desperately struggled to keep the craft steady, but it was a hopeless task. The narrows were almost upon them and she just didn't have the strength to steer the raft away from the rocky outcrop.

'Samuel,' she yelled. 'Leave that God damn gun and get back here!'

He was on the point of changing the magazine, but her unexpected use of his given name grabbed his full attention. Without even realizing the mortal danger ahead, he scrambled back to her and seized hold of the heavy pole. Together they heaved against it with all their strength, straining against the powerful current. As the ungainly craft finally began to respond, Bairstow glanced down at her and winked. She responded with a brief, but heart-warming smile. By now both of them were drenched with spray from the churning river and it was still touch and go. Then, with barely inches to spare, they swept past the cliff and Kirsty was suddenly screaming at him to swing the rudder in the opposite direction.

'Make up your mind, girl,' he bellowed out, but even as

the words left his mouth, he knew that she had the right of it. They needed to pull into the bank or be swept off down-river, leaving Bronson all alone to handle the rebels.

Marcel heard the shotgun blast down in the trees, but chose to ignore it. Whatever that was about, they still had to stop the raft and the Gatling had ceased firing. Leaping to his feet, he shouted at his two accomplices, 'The bastard's empty. Gun them down before he reloads!'

Together they peered over the cliff, rifles ready, but all they saw was the empty Missouri River. '*Mon dieu*, they are past us,' shouted the Metis leader in horrified frustration, but then he turned and observed the raft gliding into the riverbank on calmer waters. Relief flooded over him. Now they had them!

As the timber craft carrying the two young people none too gently struck the earthen bank, the US marshal stepped out on to open ground and stared up at the remaining gunmen. Immediately recognizing the threat to his otherwise occupied companions, he raised the scattergun and fired once. The deadly load struck flesh and bone and also served to distract attention from the temporarily defenceless raft. The stricken rebel tumbled down the steep rocky slope and slammed into hard earth a few yards away. His bloodied body twitched and jerked uncontrollably in its death throes. The man hadn't even cried out. As two rifles opened up on him from above, Bronson hollered over to the Mountie. 'Stop messing about with boats and get that Gatling working!'

Marcel and his one remaining crony hunkered down as they returned the lawman's unexpected fire. In the grip of desperation fuelled by fear, they feverishly worked the actions of their rifles. The hastily aimed shots went wild, but nevertheless forced the lawman to seek cover. He cursed fluently as splinters and bits of bark flew at him.

Over on the raft, Bairstow was desperately attempting to elevate the heavy gun sufficiently to pepper the cliff top. The multiple barrels were contained within a swivel, set atop the tripod that had been secured to the timber back in Alder Gulch. It required all of his considerable weight at the rear of it, to finally get them to bear on the two gunmen. He grabbed hold of the crank handle at about the same moment that Marcel remembered the deadly threat on his flank. Even as he screamed out a warning, the stream of lead caught the two of them and literally tore them apart.

Struck repeatedly by the heavy bullets, Labeau's deputy lost his footing and pitched backwards over the cliff edge. He was dead before he hit the water, but the unrelenting current swept him off in the direction taken by his leader the previous day. The other Metis merely collapsed in a blood-soaked heap on the rock and lay still.

With a great sigh of relief, the Mountie slowly allowed the heavy barrels to drop down to a horizontal position. His vision was now obscured by a huge cloud of sulphurous smoke, but ever the professional he immediately replaced the magazine with a full one.

'We've done it,' yelled Kirsty jubilantly. 'We've really done it.'

Marshal Bronson strode cautiously out from the cover of the trees. 'Maybe so,' he allowed with a wide smile. 'But it would still behove us to check all the cadavers.'

'*Behoves* is it?' laughed the Mountie elatedly. 'Have you joined the cavalry now?'

At that very moment of triumph, a single gunshot rang out. The federal officer staggered under a great blow and then collapsed heavily to the ground. Only a few yards away, a swaying blood-spattered individual stood with a smoking gun. He had only just survived the earlier shotgun blast and appeared to be too far-gone to realize the mortal danger that he was now in.

With a howl of pure rage, Samuel Bairstow swivelled the Gatling around and cranked the handle with demonic speed. Under such savage treatment the weapon soon seized up, but not before Bronson's first victim had been viciously cut down for good. With a heartfelt cry of anguish, Kirsty dashed over towards the fallen marshal.

'Please God, don't let him be dead,' she begged breathlessly.

CHAPTER ELEVEN

'Get that God damned blade away from me!' His voice was shaky, but there was no doubting the fire and determination in his words. Jesse Bronson, naked from the waist up, was lying face down on his well-worn coat next to a roaring blaze. The bullet that had laid him low was lodged in his left shoulder and required extracting.

Bairstow had heated his knife blade in the hot embers, before cooling it down again in the river. He had reluctantly agreed with himself that the unpleasant task should be his, but now he was nervous and sweating heavily. The flesh around the wound was angry and inflamed. Pretty much like the marshal himself.

'Look at you,' that man barked. 'Your hand's shaking like a greenhorn's. Like as not you'll butcher me like a steer and still miss the poxy bullet.'

Kirsty had heard enough. 'Now you just hush, marshal. Any fool can see that that lead needs to come out.' Her eyes were suddenly flooded with tears. 'We waited too long with my pa. The same is not going to happen to you. Do you hear me?'

She suddenly realized that she was shouting and that both lawmen were gazing at her in wide-eyed surprise. 'Well it's not,' she affirmed. 'Now let's get this done.' So saying, she dropped down in front of Bronson and tightly clasped his single hand.

'Put this between his teeth,' instructed Bairstow as he handed her the leather sheath from his knife. 'It'll stop him biting his God damn tongue off, although some might say that would be a good thing.'

Kneeling down next to them with the blade poised, the Mountie hesitated. 'This is going to hurt some,' he mumbled apologetically.

'Just do it!' hissed Kirsty impatiently and so he did. As the sharp point suddenly probed his tender flesh, Bronson groaned in renewed agony. Beads of sweat sprang from his forehead and his dark eyes locked feverishly on to Kirsty's. The marshal's grip on her hands was like a vice and she had to stop herself from crying out. Desperately conscious of the distress that he was causing, Bairstow eased the blade deeper until abruptly it came up against a solid object.

'I've found it,' he announced in a hushed whisper.

By now the whole of Bronson's torso was damp with sweat. The veins bulged in his neck, but somehow he managed to remain still long enough to allow the Canadian to do his job. With a triumphant cry, he held up his bloodied fingers to display a misshapen piece of lead. Dropping the knife, he commanded, 'Keep hold of him a moment longer.'

Producing a small flask from his pocket, the Mountie unscrewed the top. After taking a generous swig, he then carefully poured the contents over the livid wound. 'I was saving that for a cold night,' he remarked regretfully as Bronson squirmed under the cleansing effects of the strong alcohol. 'It was real sipping liquor.'

With his immediate torment mercifully over, the marshal

felt himself drifting into blissful unconsciousness. A dreamy look came into his eyes as he continued to stare at the young lady before him. 'Real fine country out here,' he softly remarked. 'Be a shame if it filled up with . . .' And then he was gone.

'So what do you think?' enquired Bairstow jubilantly.

Kirsty had been waiting curiously on the rest of her patient's unexpectedly sentimental comment and so glanced up at him testily. 'About what?'

'That bit of doctoring, of course,' responded the touchingly hopeful Mountie. 'I did good, didn't I?'

She looked at his bluff, cheerful face and her manner immediately softened. 'Yeah, Samuel, you did good. But if he's going to recover, he needs to be kept warm. It's going to be bitterly cold tonight. Let's bandage that shoulder and get him dressed.'

Together the two of them eased the oblivious lawman back into his well-worn duds. Struggling to get a sleeve over the vicious iron hook, Kirsty pondered, 'I wonder how he lost that hand?'

'Probably at cards, knowing him,' Bairstow responded with an uncharacteristically rapid wit.

The woman shook her head with mock despair. 'I can see I'm going to have to watch you,' she retorted swiftly. 'Are all you mounted policemen like this?'

'Only the good-looking ones,' he answered with a broad smile.

She stared fixedly at him for a moment, before suddenly favouring him with a dazzling grin that to his eyes seemed to light up the entire campsite. It abruptly occurred to him that however bitterly cold and unpleasant it got that night, there was nowhere else in the world that he'd rather be.

Jacques Labeau would not have admitted it to anybody, but he was seriously on edge. His body felt as though all the nerve ends were on fire. The reason was quite simple. He didn't like towns. Not even frontier towns and especially not those filled with Yankees. He was used to the sparsely populated northern plains, where you could ride all day without seeing another soul. Alder Gulch had been full of people of course, but that was different. He had been in total control then, at least until that damned marshal had shown up.

It was the day following his abandonment of Marcel and the second raft. His own vessel was tied up to a crude wharf on the south side of the first waterfall. He had left his two remaining men standing guard over the crates of gold and had walked in to the town of Great Falls in the Territory of Montana. The settlement had only been established two years earlier and it showed. Although it had most of the buildings required for modern living: lumber yard, bank, flower mill, schoolhouse and general store etc., the structures were all of a fairly rudimentary design and were evidently brand new. However, the community was quite obviously large enough to support many hundreds of settlers, which meant that he would have to tread carefully.

Many of the citizens glanced curiously at him as he trudged along the muddy thoroughfare. It was unusual for strangers to be on foot. The only way to achieve that was to travel on the river and very few arrived by raft in winter. Studiously ignoring the gawkers, Labeau kept moving until he located what he was looking for.

The livery was the largest building in town. Its owner, one Taylor Racine, regarded the half-breed with a complete lack of enthusiasm and a sizeable amount of suspicion. He took in the jet-black hair, the high cheekbones and more particularly the well-worn repeating rifle and decided that he didn't like the newcomer. He didn't like him one little bit.

'What can *you* do for *me*, stranger?' Racine pointedly enquired with an unusual twist to the normal greeting. He was a large, well-fed individual who made a point of always wearing a revolver. That was uncommon, because Great Falls was a peaceful town and the once fearsome Blackfeet Indians were no longer any threat. But horse stealing was not completely unknown in the territory and nobody thieved from Taylor Racine without risking a bloody death.

The Metis fought down his immediate anger at the man's hostility. He didn't possess enough force to take what he wanted, so he would just have to negotiate. 'I need the use of two strong wagons and two teams to pull them. There's no risk for you, because they won't even be leaving town by much.'

'I'll be the judge of the risk,' responded Racine acidly. 'What are you shifting and how long do you want them for?'

Labeau was ready for that. 'Crates of high grade ore samples. They're up river on a raft. How long depends on when the next steamboat arrives.'

Racine just could not resist a sneering response. 'Ore samples! What does a breed know about grading rocks?'

The rebel leader could feel his pulse racing, as an all too familiar rage began to build within him. People had died for far less. His left eye twitched slightly as his manic gaze settled on the livery owner. 'You would be wise not to press me, Yankee, or I'll forget that we have business to discuss.'

The American's eyes narrowed thoughtfully, as he absorbed the uncompromising response. To him, the stranger had the look of dangerous border trash and there was no telling just how many more of them might be in the area. He suddenly decided that it might, after all, be best to humour him for a while. 'You could well be in luck,' he remarked in a more agreeable tone. 'The next steamer's due tomorrow, unless the boiler explodes or the fool captain grounds her in the shallows. That should give you time to portage these *rocks* of yours. Once I've seen the *colour* of your money, of course.'

Racine's hinting at the possible presence of gold did not go unnoticed, but Labeau chose to ignore it and instead produced an enticing selection of Yankee dollars and greenbacks from his pockets. The livery owner's transformation of mood was apparently complete. It was time for some civilized negotiation and then the breed could have his wagons. Or at least he would until the businessman had the chance to round up some armed men from the community!

'Well, well, just what have we got here?' Nelson Pruitt gazed with rapt attention through his battered drawtube spyglass. It had been the only thing of value that he had inherited from his father, a fast-talking riverboat gambler shot dead for cheating at cards. The scratched lenses enabled him to view the swarthy figure of Jacques Labeau, as that man rode towards the river on his newly acquired wagon. Shifting the glass over to his left, Pruitt swiftly spotted the heavily laden raft and its two guards. Raising his voice, he stated, 'Looks like we've got a pay day coming.'

Dutch Henry Bruckner was by his side in an instant. 'Say what?' he demanded belligerently. In fairness to the huge man, such a condition was his natural state, but now it was heightened because of the extreme tension that had developed within the small group. The shoulder wound sustained by the colourfully named Black Bart had become infected during their gruelling journey from Alder Gulch. All that bitter morning, he had been feverishly wailing and mumbling, to the point where Dutch Henry desperately wanted to put a ball in his skull. He had been forcefully dissuaded by the fourth member of the gang, a certain Jackson Pyke. That man had graphically threatened to exchange shots if anyone attempted to dispatch his long-term trail buddy. The four men were now ensconced in the trees on a hillside overlooking Great Falls.

Handing the spyglass over, Pruitt remarked, 'I'd bet my back teeth that those crates are packed with ill-gotten gold.'

Dutch Henry stared fixedly at the raft for a few moments. 'So let's get down there and take it off them. Three poxy half-breeds aren't going to stop me and I've got a powerful need to kill something.' He glanced pointedly back at their two companions before turning his attention to Nelson Pruitt. That man selected his words carefully. Contradicting the huge outlaw could have fatal consequences, but he had some good reasons for doing so.

'Labeau will be waiting for a steamboat to arrive. Why not let him do all the hard work before we move in. And,' he continued conspiratorially, 'The young man that you butchered, said that there were two rafts loaded with gold. It would make sense to see if that turns up before showing our hand.' He nodded encouragingly as he waited for Dutch Henry's response. When it came, it turned out to be surprisingly painful.

The big man regarded him sullenly for some time, before finally coming to a decision. Suddenly reaching out a huge paw, he brought it down with stunning force on Pruitt's back. 'You know, you're not as stupid as you look. Yeah, all right. We'll wait on events, but if he doesn't stop that God damn wailing, I'm going to get to whittling again!'

It was early that same afternoon when Jesse Bronson finally opened his eyes. He groaned at the strong light shafting in from the low winter sun and hastily closed them. Lying under his thick coat, he could feel the heat from a roaring fire nearby and had not the slightest inclination to move. It was the tempting aroma of food that eventually convinced him to try again. He cautiously allowed his eyelids to form slits and took a look around. What he saw brought a chuckle to his lips. The Mountie had lifted the Gatling gun off its tripod and was attempting to clear the blockage.

'Ha,' the wounded man rasped. 'First time you've used that big beast and you managed to break it!'

'Whilst saving your life,' Bairstow quickly countered. 'And it's not broken. There's a spent cartridge wedged in here, is all. I'll soon have it out.'

'Well you had better be quick,' Bronson retorted. 'Because we're burning daylight.'

Kirsty's trim form suddenly appeared at the marshal's side. There was a glow to her features that hadn't existed the day before and she winked at the Mountie, before turning her full attention to the wounded officer. Favouring him with a sharp glance, she shook her head. 'You're not going anywhere, Marshal Bronson. You've got vittles to eat and you need lots of rest. That wound doesn't look like it wants to infect, but I've got to keep it clean and change the bandage.'

If she had thought that her argument would intimidate Jesse Bronson, then she was sadly mistaken. 'Anything you need to do to me, you can do on that damned raft,' he asserted forcefully. 'If that bull turd, Labeau, has reached Great Falls, then he'll be looking out for a paddle steamer. Once he and the gold are on one, we've lost him for good. And that redcoat and I have come too far to see that happen. So I'm going to eat the food that you've kindly prepared, but *then* you're going to help me get my possibles together and we're back on the river. Bairstow, am I going to have any trouble with you? You know that I'm right!'

The Mountie had stopped tinkering with the gun and was regarding him thoughtfully. Then, glancing apologetically at the young woman, he answered, 'Yeah. I hate to say it, but he's right, Kirsty. Only thing is, what do we do with this load of gold? We can't abandon it for any passing scavengers.'

'We take it with us and leave our raft here. Anybody who finds that is welcome to it,' came Bronson's heartfelt response.

Bairstow was appalled. 'But if Labeau gets the better of us, then we have given him the gold back.'

'So you'd better get that gun working again then, hadn't you. No one said that this was going to be easy. It strikes me that you must have led a sheltered life up there in Canada.'

By way of response to the marshal's sarcastic comment, the Mountie triumphantly prized a bent cartridge case out of the Gatling's mechanism and tossed it into the fire close to Bronson's prone figure. 'If that was a live round, you'd be leaping about a bit, wouldn't you *old man*.' With that, he heaved the heavy weapon into his arms and carried it over to the captured raft.

Kirsty at least had the good grace to admit defeat. 'I

reckon Great Falls just doesn't know what's going to hit it, come tomorrow.'

She couldn't possibly have known just how prescient that comment was!

CHAPTER TWELVE

Captain Jacob Stuckey, master and pilot of the riverboat *Ethan Allen*, peered curiously down from his perch in the pilothouse at the two approaching wagons. His men were busy tying off the paddle steamer to the pile driven posts on the riverbank. He and his one hundred and ninety feet long vessel had just completed the protracted and arduous trip from Bismarck, Dakota Territory, on a section of what was the longest and most dangerous river in the USA. All he wanted was to sleep the clock round, but there was something about the potential customers that troubled him. They were quite obviously half-breeds and armed to the teeth. And looking at the wagon springs, the cargo had to be unusually heavy. Stuckey knew trouble when he saw it and they were just that.

'Mr Martin,' he bellowed out to his second officer. 'Those men don't set foot on this boat until I get down there!'

'It's time!' Nelson Pruitt had watched the paddle steamer, with its two towering smokestacks, nestle up to the riverbank. Jacques Labeau's heavily laden wagons were rolling smartly towards it. 'Oh, it's time all right'.

Dutch Henry and Jackson Pyke were mounted with guns ready, impatient to kill someone, anyone. All the men had passed a desperately uncomfortable night on the hillside, eschewing even a small telltale fire and sustained mainly by the thought of so much gold. They knew that with only three of the Canadians remaining, negotiations were no longer necessary. There might even be a bonus, if the scalp of the rebel leader were to carry a bounty.

The ill-fated Black Bart was too far-gone to take part in anything. With a mortified shoulder, he was wrapped in a saddle-blanket, burning up with fever. His would be a protracted, but inevitable death. The fact that Pyke had faithfully promised to return may have provided a little comfort, but would not in any way change the outcome.

'One last look around,' insisted Pruitt as he mounted up. It was then that everything started to go wrong. As his glass swept away from the landing and off towards the first of the waterfalls to the west of the town, he chanced upon a group of armed men emerging from the livery. 'Looks like someone else has their eye on the prize,' he remarked with sudden agitation. And it only got worse. Where the abandoned raft had languished, there were suddenly two, only this second one had a load of crates and a Gatling gun on it. More gold, yes, but it was accompanied by two very unwelcome lawmen.

'Sweet Jesus! Bronson's down there,' he howled. 'That man just won't die.'

'This doesn't sit well with me, Taylor,' muttered one of the men doubtfully. 'I ain't no gun hand and those fellers haven't done anything to us.'

Taylor Racine rounded on him in disgust. 'You see those

wagons?' he demanded, pointing vaguely in the direction of the river. 'They're my wagons and my horses and I know exactly what's going down here. Those sons of bitches are going to roll straight on to the steamer and sashay on down the Missouri. That'll be the last I see of any of it and all I'll have to balance my ledgers is a stinking raft, fit only for kindling. You think I'm going to stand for that? Well do you?'

The spokesman paled under the big man's anger and glanced around at his fellows for support. There were seven of them including Racine and all of them in some way were beholden to the livery owner for a living, either as employees or those who depended upon the availability of his wagons. They all, rather self-consciously, had revolvers strapped to their waists and three of them carried Winchesters. None of them, including their leader, could be classed as gunfighters, but living out west they all knew how to shoot.

One of the townsfolk, a burly freighter called Wilson, spoke for the majority. 'I'm in no itching hurry to get into a gunfight, but hell, Tyler, there's only three undersized breeds out there. Seems to me if we put on a good show they'll just melt away, back where they came from and we'll get to share in whatever's in those crates. There won't even be any killing.'

The others nodded their support and so it was that the unofficial posse left the livery and headed purposefully towards Captain Stuckey's sternwheeler.

With great relief, Jesse Bronson clambered off the raft and began to get his bearings. His shoulder ached abominably and his left arm was temporarily useless. Samuel Bairstow had stripped the Metis dead of their leather belts and had fashioned a very serviceable sling for him. Remarkably, Kirsty seemed to have developed a form of motherly affection for him, because she was forever fiddling with his coat or gently touching his arm.

'Hell's teeth, girl, unhand me! This isn't the first time I've been shot, you know. How do you think I lost my hand? It wasn't eaten by a grizzly.' But as he barked out the words, he favoured her with a smile, because in truth it had been a long time since anyone had fussed over him and he was growing to like it.

Bairstow checked the loads in the sawn-off and then handed it over to the marshal. 'How do you read it, Deputy?'

That man gazed up at the surrounding hills for a moment, before suddenly fixing his steely eyes on the young woman. 'I suppose there's no point in telling you to stay here, is there?'

'Damn right, there isn't,' she declared. 'You won't be using your Winchester for a while, so I reckon I'll just lay claim to it.'

'That's what I figured,' responded Bronson with a hint of pride. '*And,* since there are three horsemen heading full chisel off that hillside, I say we leave this God damn raft, the gold and the big gun and head into town, pronto!'

His two companions twisted around to follow his gaze. 'Just who could they be?' pondered the Mountie.

The marshal was fumbling in his pockets, searching vainly for his field glasses. It pained him to think that they might have ended up in the river. 'Couldn't make them out, but when did strangers ever bring anything but trouble?'

Labeau, his eyes fixed on the captain coming down from the pilothouse to meet him, still somehow sensed the group of men moving up behind him. He briefly hoped that it would be Marcel and the crew of the second raft, but was destined to be disappointed. As his glance took in the assorted townsfolk, the Canadian nodded to himself with grim acceptance. Without a word, he dropped down from the wagon's bench seat and turned to meet the threat. He recognized Racine in the lead, with the various rabble following on behind and instinctively knew what to do. The time for talking with the big windbag was now past. 'Stay with the wagons,' he instructed his men.

The Metis leader slowly placed his hand on his revolver and moved directly towards the seven men. As the gap closed to mere feet, Taylor Racine displayed momentary indecision and came to a halt. 'Now see here, mister,' he began. 'We don't want any trouble, but you ain't. . . .'

Without breaking stride, Labeau drew, cocked and fired his revolver directly into Racine's face. That man's head snapped back under the shocking impact and, almost in slow motion, his body crumpled to the ground, blood gushing from his wrecked features.

Abruptly leaderless, the rest of the group froze in the face of such brutal violence. That response wasn't nearly enough for Labeau, who wanted rid of them entirely. Veering off to his left, he arrived on their flank and opened fire at point blank range. The reluctant Tyler took a bullet in the neck and fell to his knees, gagging on his own blood. As sulphurous smoke began to obscure the nightmarish scene, another man was struck in the upper arm and yet another in the chest. Seemingly incapable of responding to the deadly enfilade fire, the makeshift posse simply fell to pieces. Those that could hightailed it for the livery, leaving the wounded to their own devices. Not so much as a single shot had been discharged by Racine's party.

So secure was he in his effortless victory that the single gunman stood his ground and casually replaced the empty cartridges, completely impervious to the cries of pain around him. It was only when one of his companions bellowed over to him that he displayed any concern. 'Riders, Jacques. Coming in fast!'

Sure enough, he heard the rapid pounding of hoofs. Since the newcomers were an unknown quantity, Labeau turned and raced back to the wagons.

The three horsemen charged into Great Falls and then, on reaching the first buildings, abruptly reined in. Nelson Pruitt addressed his two cronies. 'Those half-breeds know me, so once we come up with them we'll dismount and get close. Maybe get the drop on them.' So saying, he moved off at a walk and led the way along the muddy thoroughfare towards the landing. Dutch Henry said nothing, but there was a noticeable tightening around his jaw line. He was getting tired of taking instructions. In his opinion Nelson, although undeniably quick-witted, was not half the man that Taylor Pruitt had been until he had got shot to pieces by Bronson's sawn-off.

Even though it was a cold day, there were many citizens on the streets, drawn to the unexpected sound of gunfire. They looked up curiously as the three trail worn riders passed by. Those men glanced dismissively at each face as they drew nearer to the *Ethan Allen*'s two smokestacks. They'd heard gunfire on the way in and so the scene that greeted them provided no surprises. On the open land between the town proper and the landing area, four men were on the ground. Two were quite obviously dead, with another apparently breathing his last. The fourth was cradling a bloodied arm, whilst desperately trying to get to his feet.

Pruitt came to an abrupt halt and the others followed suit. Directly facing them was the Missouri River with the big steamboat moored at its edge, smoke still lazily drifting out of the two stacks. In front of that were the two wagons containing an untold fortune. The three men slowly dismounted and gazed longingly at the crates. Dutch Henry licked his lips in anticipation – although whether that was at the prospect of the money or more bloodletting was anybody's guess.

The Metis leader's piercing gaze settled on the three newcomers and for a moment he was uncharacteristically confused. 'Pruitt! What the hell brings you here?' he called out. Then, before the other man could reply, everything suddenly became very clear. The *cochon* had been to Alder Gulch and someone had talked.

Nelson Pruitt managed to impose the makings of a smile on his grubby face. It was days since he had dragged a razor across his flesh and so the greeting showed as more of a grimace. 'Well hello again, Mr Labeau. Looks like we've just arrived in time to help with the loading. This big fellow next to me will prove mighty handy when it comes to lifting.'

Mr Labeau took in the singularly menacing behemoth and knew that such a man would only ever wish to impose his will on others. With the unfortunate parity in numbers, it was obvious that Pruitt and his cronies had not come to assist, but to take. Brandishing his reloaded revolver, the Metis whispered to his two men, 'Be ready,' before responding to Pruitt's *kind* offer. 'Any of you sons of bitches makes a move towards us and he'll end up in a box. That's if you've got the price of a coffin!'

The ragged smile completely slipped from Pruitt's face. 'That's what I call real unfriendly. Do you hear that, fellas? We ride all this way to make an honest dollar, only to have our help thrown back in our faces.' Even as he spoke, his mind was considering the possibilities. With the Metis sheltering behind two wagons, a shootout could only go badly. The best time to make their move would be when Labeau attempted to get the wagons on to the paddle steamer.

'Are we going to take these pus weasels or what?' demanded Dutch Henry impatiently. He was just itching to trigger his massive Colt Dragoon, but Pruitt shook his head firmly.

'They've got nowhere to go, except on that riverboat. That's when they'll be vulnerable and that's when we'll take them.' With that, he began to slowly back away. His two companions had no choice other than to follow him.

Labeau snorted disdainfully. He knew exactly what the Yankees were about. 'Keep your guns on them, while I parley with this captain,' he commanded.

Jacob Stuckey proved easy to locate. He and a number of his thirty crewmen were standing on the covered deck, forward of the deckhouse, observing the edgy confrontation with uneasy interest. The captain was a burly, bearded individual with twenty years' experience on the Missouri River. In his time he had encountered many ruffians and was not easily cowed, but nevertheless regretted leaving his carbine in the pilothouse.

'We've got some cargo for you,' began Labeau reasonably. 'If you'll get some planking down, we'll lead the first wagon onboard. They'll need to be thick, mind. There's some weight here.'

Stuckey's reply was swift and to the point. 'I'm not doing anything until you answer to the law for those killings. Racine was not an easy man to like, but you've got his wagons and his animals, so he must have had reason to come after you.' Turning his head, he whispered hurriedly to the nearest crewman. 'Tell the engine room to get up a head of steam and then fetch my Sharps. Keep to the far side of the boat, mind!'

That man blinked in surprise, but nevertheless swivelled on his heels to comply. Labeau witnessed the murmured aside, and chose to react with murderous intent. Again drawing his revolver, he aimed directly at the crewman's broad back and fired. The stricken individual vomited a stream of blood and pitched forward on to a coil of rope. As he twitched uncontrollably, his killer switched his smoking weapon on to the suddenly outraged captain.

'You murdering scoundrel! There was no call to do that. He wasn't even armed!'

Labeau was mercilessly unrepentant. 'Armed. Unarmed. What's the difference? It's obvious you've taken against me, but if you don't do as I say, then you'll be next for a bullet!'

'I ain't never seen shooting like it, Marshal. Honest I ain't. I thought I was a goner for sure. He was like the very devil!' The freighter, Wilson, had survived the terrifying encounter with Labeau and had an adrenaline charged compulsion to recount his story for the very welcome new arrivals. Bronson and his two companions had heard the rapid gunfire on their way from the raft. By the time that they had reached their current vantage point, Pruitt and his cronies had backed off, so that only the *Ethan Allen* and the wagons were visible to him. Impatiently the lawman cut the freighter off short and so never heard the whereabouts of the three other menacing strangers.

'Who's the captain of that riverboat?'

Wilson didn't have to give that any thought. 'It'll be Jacob Stuckey. He always does the run up from Bismarck.'

'Stuckey!' exclaimed the lawman. 'I know that old river rat. He's one tough *hombre*. It could work to our advantage.' With that, he took another look around the corner of the building and was just in time to witness Labeau's shooting of the crewman.

'By Christ,' exclaimed Bairstow. 'That was outright murder.'

'Damn right it was,' replied a strangely calm Marshal Bronson. 'And it changes everything. We are no longer trying to just arrest and deport that bastard. My first duty now is to protect the lives of those river men.'

Kirsty gazed at him pensively. It occurred to her that her friends in Alder Gulch had more on their minds than maintaining law and order. They just wanted their gold back. And yet she was sensible enough to hold her tongue, because justice for the death of her father also figured in the young woman's thinking.

'So what's your plan?' demanded the Mountie. 'You always seem to have one!'

'It just so happens that I do,' responded Bronson, who must have done some mighty quick thinking. Patting his shotgun, he continued with, 'I'm no use with a long gun right now. I need to get up close with this scattergun. So sad to relate, it looks like Kirsty and I are going for another Missouri boat ride.'

CHAPTER THIRTEEN

Jacob Stuckey stood impotently by as his commandeered crewmen heaved out a massive makeshift drawbridge. The timbers were thick and gnarled, as they would need to be to take the weight of the wagons. His foul temper was not improved by the feel of the gun muzzle rammed into the back of his neck. The frustrated captain was well aware just how thin Labeau's forces were spread. He and his men outnumbered them ten to one. Unfortunately the crew were all unarmed. The days of river pirates had mostly past, so the only weapons were kept up in the pilothouse and he was under no illusions as to just how ruthless the Metis leader could be. The fresh pool of blood on the deck testified to that.

As the *Ethan Allen*'s crew commenced to lead the first team on to the planking, Dutch Henry Bruckner began to shake with barely suppressed rage. 'If we don't make a move soon, you maggot, they're going to get clean away. All that spondulix has got to be worth taking a risk for.'

Nelson Pruitt stared up at the huge man with a mixture of exasperation and fear. So far, he had been able to maintain a tenuous control by employing a mixture of quick wits and logic, but that time had passed. Now was the time for sheer bloody violence. Yet, preferring gunplay of a more one-sided kind, his guts churned at the thought of assaulting well-armed men stationed behind thick timber. He just couldn't think what to do and his frightening companion sensed that indecision.

'You poxy little cur,' snarled Dutch Henry. 'Stay here then, but don't expect any handouts after it's over.' Switching his gaze to Jackson Pyke, he demanded, 'Well, are you with me or what?'

That man glanced from one to the other, before nodding slowly. 'I signed on knowing there might be killing and nothing's changed.'

A rare smile trickled across Dutch Henry's brutalized features. 'Let's get to it th—'

The shot that rang out from off to their left took everybody by surprise. The bullet thwacked into the rear wagon, kicking off a large splinter and narrowly missing one of Labeau's men.

'Didn't think those livery fellas would have the grit to come back for more,' remarked Pyke.

'Sweet Jesus,' Pruitt exclaimed. Until that moment he had quite forgotten the arrival of the lawmen at the far side of town. 'Livery men, my arse! That's God damned Bronson!'

Kirsty eased the little rowing boat up against the side of the *Ethan Allen*. Bronson, his grubby trousers now slimy with bilge water, balanced precariously in the centre of the unstable craft. White-faced at being on water yet again, he didn't even possess a hand to assist with his balance. One arm was still tightly bound, whilst his right hand gripped the stock of his shotgun. Although desperate to clamber up on to the steamboat's solid deck, the lawman controlled his impatience and cautiously peered over the wooden rail. What he saw gave him little solace.

Halfway across the deck, two men stood in almost indecent proximity. To the fore was Jacob Stuckey, but he was partially concealed by a swarthy individual who had a revolver pressed to the captain's neck. Any shot would have to be shrewdly judged and certainly not taken with a scattergun. Mind made up, Bronson turned slightly and carefully handed the big gun over to Kirsty. Then, drawing his Remington, he leaned his torso against the side rail and took careful aim at Labeau's left leg. Anywhere else risked also penetrating the helpless captive. And yet he still couldn't fire. Not unless he wanted to risk Stuckey taking a fatal bullet from the contraction of a wounded man's trigger finger. Despite the cold, sweat began to flow freely as the lawman maintained his aim.

'God damn it, Bairstow,' he railed silently. 'Trigger that long gun!'

As though with divine providence, there was a crash over near the stables and a bullet struck the rear wagon. Instinctively, Labeau swept his weapon over to face a new threat and Bronson took his chance. The Remington bucked satisfyingly in his hand. With a howl of agony, Labeau dropped to one knee. As blood began to seep from that man's leg, Bronson holstered his smoking revolver, reached back for the shotgun and bellowed out, 'It's Jesse Bronson. Arm yourself, Jacob!'

Stuckey tore away from his captor's weakened grasp and made for the steps leading up to the pilothouse. Labeau, struggling to regain his footing, desperately wanted to shoot the fleeing captain, but knew that he was threatened by a far deadlier foe. Grimacing with pain, he threw himself forward and around the side of the deckhouse. 'The law dog's on the boat,' he bellowed out to his two men.

Another shot rang out from the livery and the Metis near the rear wagon ducked down before returning fire. His companion had been in the process of supervising the arrival of the first team aboard and the wagon was literally on the planking, neither ashore nor aboard ship. As the first shot rang out, the crew fled for the stern, leaving the heavy conveyance to its own devices. They were soon safely hidden from the rest of the deck by the vast cords of wood, used to feed the three boilers down below, that were stacked all around. When Bronson appeared at the far side of the steamer, the lone Metis was attempting in vain to calm the horses and only belatedly drew his belt gun. He was hopelessly outmatched.

The sawn-off belched its deadly load, which caught him in the face and chest, but also struck the nearest horse. The Canadian rebel, suddenly out of his mind with pain, staggered back against the side rail and then toppled over into the freezing water. Simultaneously, the wounded animal whinnied pitifully and vainly sought to escape its sudden agony. Straining against the heavy load, it leapt to the side and collided with the other lead horse. The two behind had no choice other than to follow on and so the heavily laden wagon suddenly veered off the stout planking, plunged into the narrow gap between ship and shore and in so doing dragged the hapless beasts with it.

The massive tie ropes securing the vessel held and so inevitably the conveyance became wedged tight. As night follows day, the crates of gold overwhelmed the wagon sides and plummeted into the Missouri River. The noise from the four horses was stupendous as they kicked the *Ethan Allen*'s wooden rail into pieces, in a desperate bid to keep their footing.

Viewing all this mayhem from the opposite side of the deck, Bronson couldn't resist taunting the rebel leader. 'Looks like your ill-gotten gains are slipping away from you, Frenchie.'

Jacques Labeau was beside himself with pain and anger. 'You'll pay for this, you Yankee bastard!' With that he fired wildly round the corner of the deckhouse, but the marshal had already shifted position.

Bronson knelt down on the deck and awkwardly replaced the spent cartridge in each weapon. Then he peered over the side and hissed at Kirsty. 'I'm going round the back. You cover this side with that long gun and *be careful!*' Without waiting for a response, he padded off down the deck, sawn-off cocked and ready.

The surviving Metis crouched down behind the second wagon and swore fluently as yet another rifle bullet smashed into the timber next to him. With the gangway blocked by four crazed animals, he was not about to retreat that way and he didn't dare vault the side rail whilst that cursed Yankee was taking well aimed pot shots at him. Then he finally witnessed something that made him smile. The three gunhands that had tried jawboning with Labeau were racing on foot towards the livery. It appeared as though the sharpshooter was about to get an unwelcome surprise.

Up in the pilothouse, Jacob Stuckey grabbed hold of the old Sharps breech-loading carbine that had been there for years. It did not have the outright speed of a repeater, but it was exceedingly accurate and had occasionally proved to be very useful in settling trouble on the river. And now his old friend Jesse Bronson was on the boat and it seemed like the marshal had a deputy over near the livery stables. It was then that he too spotted the three men making for that exact spot. They were moving fast, which meant that he had to as well.

Retracting the hammer, Jacob drew a bead on the point man, which just happened to be Jackson Pyke. The riverboat captain knew that whatever transpired, the noise of his shot might at least attract the deputy's attention. With his powerful carbine aimed just slightly in front of the running man, he squeezed the trigger. Responding with an encouraging roar, the gun jerked against his shoulder and Pyke appeared to trip mid stride.

Down below, the Metis heard the loud report and glanced around at the pilothouse. He saw Stuckey with the smoking carbine and, perhaps unwisely, moved away from the wagon. Labeau might have hesitated, knowing that they would need the captain on any trip down river, but his minion possessed no such intelligence. Instinctively raising his revolver, he blasted off three rapid shots. The first one struck timber, the second and third flesh and blood. Jacob Stuckey crashed back against the rear of the small building, before sliding painfully to the floor. Blood trickled out of his mouth and the carbine slipped from his grasp.

'You moron,' screamed the rebel leader from the side of the deckhouse. 'We needed him!'

After Bronson and Kirsty had left him, Corporal Bairstow had relocated to the livery. Although not the nearest building to the landing area, it allowed space to fire and move and offered some good vantage points. He got off a number of shots at the remaining wagon and heard the muted roar of a shotgun on the far side of the steamer. It was as the Mountie settled down amongst the hay bales in the loft overlooking the stables that he heard a different report, followed by a cry of pain outside.

'That sounded like a buffalo gun,' he muttered. His Winchester was poking through a large chink in the timber. Deciding to temporarily ignore events outside, he glanced down the barrel at the riverboat, just in time to witness Stuckey's death. His killer had risen up behind the wagon to fire the shots, presenting Bairstow with a temptingly perfect target. Drawing a fine bead, the lawman smoothly squeezed the trigger. He didn't even need to see his smoke-obscured victim to know that the bullet had flown true. And besides, he suddenly had little time to dwell on his success.

With a tremendous crash, one of the stable doors swung back against the wall. Two guns fired simultaneously, the bullets driving up through the thin timber planking that made up the floor. Snatching his rifle out of the crack in the wall, Bairstow fired on the move for effect. Then a voice bellowed out from below. 'Cover me while I go up after the bastard!'

Heavy boots sounded on the ladder, followed by the roar of two more shots. One of the bullets came within inches of his face, as the Canadian levered in another cartridge and took aim at the top of the steps. So far he hadn't seen anyone, but that was about to change. A massive horse-pistol suddenly appeared over the top rung, mere yards away, and discharged with a deafening roar. The bullet slammed into a roof beam above his head, but it was the muzzle flash that did the damage. In the poor light, it caused him to blink rapidly, so that his answering shot also went wide. The owner of the Colt Dragoon didn't even bother to fire again. Instead he clambered into the loft and charged towards his prey.

As the huge brute closed in, Bairstow frantically worked the Winchester's under-lever. With a fresh cartridge in the firing chamber, he was just swinging the barrel into line when two enormous meaty hands grabbed it. The rifle was torn from his strong grasp with unbelievable force.

Dutch Henry Bruckner stood in the loft, his head brushing the roof. The makings of a rare smile washed over his brutal features. Brandishing the captured weapon, he backed off a few paces so as to size up his opponent. He noted Bairstow's powerful build and took in the scarlet tunic, visible under the open buffalo coat, and the grey uniform breeches.

'So you're a Mountie, huh? You must really fancy yourself, wearing that pretty red jacket an' all.'

Bairstow, still shocked at the ease with which he had lost his rifle, nevertheless squared his shoulders and provided a robustly pompous response. 'I am a Northwest Mounted Policeman in the service of the Queen and you would be well advised to stand clear!'

The great ogre looming before him merely gave out a rumble of laughter. 'Haw, haw, haw. The way I hear it, you fellows always catch your man. Well I'll tell you something. You don't look much to me. So hell, I'm not even going to use a gun on you!' With that, he casually tossed the Winchester out of the loft. His ancient Colt was stuffed back in his ample waistband as he hunched his massive shoulders and moved forward.

Down below, Nelson Pruitt smiled to himself. To his certain knowledge, Dutch Henry hadn't lost a fight since the age of fifteen, so in his opinion the deadly contest was a foregone conclusion. Accordingly, Pruitt decided that he would be of far more use looking to the gold, as it was quite possible that Labeau would find Marshal Bronson to be too much of a handful. Mind made up, he headed for the open door. In truth, he wasn't sorry to be missing the brutal clash, as he didn't much share Bruckner's enthusiasm for blood sports!

If I let this oaf get on top of me, I'm finished! With such grim thoughts preying on his mind, Bairstow realized that the use of superior speed was likely to be his only chance. Abruptly dropping to the floorboards, he kicked out viciously with both legs. Taken by surprise, his huge opponent tried to dodge, but stumbled and fell heavily on to the timber. As a cloud of dust and wood shavings descended on the stables below, the Mountie twisted around and flung himself on to his winded enemy. Sitting astride Dutch Henry's massive torso, he bunched both fists and landed two tremendous blows on that man's defenceless features. He then made a big mistake. Rather than keep pounding away, he instead tried to reach for his Adams revolver in its flap holster.

With fresh blood trickling from his mashed lips, Dutch Henry reached up and grabbed his assailant by the throat. With enormous power, he rolled over, so that the positions were rapidly reversed and it was he who was on top. Drawing back an immense fist, he slammed it down into Bairstow's unprotected face. The savage blow was like an anvil strike. The Mountie's vision blurred as a great roaring sound abruptly inhabited his skull. He tasted blood and suddenly recognized with frightening clarity that another such pile driver would quite probably kill him.

With a strength born of desperation, Bairstow drove the straight fingers of his right hand up into the big man's throat. Gagging with shock, that individual rocked backwards, allowing the other man a brief respite. Twisting like an eel, the lawman managed to break out from under the vast weight of his opponent and then kick out with his right leg. The fur-covered boot caught Bruckner in the groin, eliciting a howl of agony from him.

Getting groggily to his feet, Bairstow knew he had a chance to finish the fight. Again drawing back his right boot, he aimed a mighty kick at the outlaw's head. With mere inches left to travel, Dutch Henry unbelievably managed to reach up and grab his assailant's foot. With a tremendous heave, he tossed Bairstow back into the livery wall, but was still suffering too much to follow up on it – which was a good thing for Bairstow because the Mountie ended up back on the floor gasping for breath.

With both of them temporarily unable to move, the two combatants surveyed each other through the unlit gloom of the loft. They were bleeding profusely, but seemed not to notice. Dutch Henry spat out a great gobbet of bloodied phlegm, before rasping out, 'You fight like a woman, Mountie. That must be why they give you such pretty red jackets.'

'Go to hell, convict,' that man wheezed as he got to his feet.

'I've already been there,' replied Bruckner as he too staggered upright.

For a few moments, both men silently inhaled great draughts of air until with an eerie composure they advanced on each other again.

The marshal had instructed Kirsty to cover her side of the steamer, but she couldn't do that *and* control her footing in the small rowing boat. It remorselessly bucked and twisted under the influence of the current until finally she decided to let it drift away. Carefully placing her Winchester on the apparently deserted deck, she clambered up over the side – in the process feeling the stern counter of the little craft brush her feet as it sped away. She couldn't resist glancing at it as it bobbed up and down on the fast-flowing river. In such conditions it was probably gone for good, which to her thrifty mind seemed such a waste. Then her spine tingled as she heard a faint scuffling from behind. Instinctively reaching down for Bronson's rifle, she suddenly found it pinned to the deck by a blood-stained boot.

'So we meet again, *ma chérie*!'

In horrified silence, she peered up at Jacques Labeau's swarthy features. Her moment of daydreaming had likely cost her dear and yet how on earth had he managed to reach her so swiftly? As though sensing *and* enjoying her disquiet, he favoured her with a sardonic smile.

'It's such a shame I don't have time to benefit from this meeting, but sadly you have to leave again.' So saying, he thrust his solid body up against hers and shoved hard. Panic stricken, Kirsty felt herself falling backwards. Unable to secure any kind of handhold, the young woman plunged down into the ice-cold Missouri River.

CHAPTER FOURTEEN

Two men responded in very different ways to Kirsty's high-pitched scream. First Officer Martin heard the loud splash that accompanied it and reacted with professional speed. The *Ethan Allen* consumed as many as thirty cords of wood per day and consequently much of the fuel had to be stored on deck. Reaching towards the nearest pile of timber, he seized a large chunk and hurled it into the river with commendable accuracy. It smacked down very close to the struggling young woman.

'Grab it and paddle for the bank,' Martin somewhat unnecessarily bellowed. In his heart, he knew that her chances of survival in such cold water were slim, but he had done all that he could for the moment.

Jesse Bronson knew exactly what the scream portended. It meant that Jacques Labeau had just baited a trap for the marshal to blunder into, except of course that he wasn't having any of it. Very reluctantly accepting that the gutsy young woman was quite probably doomed, the lawman awkwardly scrambled up on to a pile of timber. From there he was able to place his shotgun on the roof of the deckhouse and then, with one hand, drag his big frame after it.

146

Barely suppressed rage coursed through his body as he moved across the wooden roof in a low crouch. It was fired by bitter anger at Labeau, but also at himself for having left a mere slip of a girl all alone in the presence of such an adversary. At least he did not have to worry too much about being heard, because the horse that he had inadvertently wounded was still pounding around on the deck. Bronson had a fair idea where the Metis would be waiting and so it proved. The Canadian rebel, who was now a leader in name only, was lurking behind a woodpile close to where Kirsty had left the boat. From the look of the dark sticky pool at his feet, his leg wound was obviously bleeding heavily.

With a mirthless smile, the marshal drew back slightly from the edge of the roof and carefully lowered his big gun on to the caulked timber. His own particular injury required him to carry out some deft manoeuvring. Extracting a set of handcuffs from his belt, he placed them between his chipped teeth and then recovered the shotgun. Turning his head sharply to the left, he then rotated it swiftly back again and opened his jaws. Without warning, the handcuffs crashed down on to the deck some eighteen inches away from Jacques Labeau. That individual's head jerked up in shock as though he had just been savagely bitten by a mule. His bloodshot eyes rotated like swivels, until they settled on the gaping muzzles of the sawn-off shotgun. Behind them stood the grim figure of a badged-up deputy US marshal.

'For myself, I'd just as soon consign you to hell,' that man remarked with chilling clarity. 'But I'm a federal officer. So you'd best put those irons on before I change my mind. Oh, and wrap your arms around that post before you do it. That way you won't get tempted to run off anywhere.'

Labeau gazed up at him with a mixture of horrified

loathing and fear. No man had ever put him in chains before, but there really wasn't any arguing with a twelve gauge. Very reluctantly, he lowered his weapon and did as instructed.

From his vantage point, Bronson could see a number of crewmen milling around near the stern and called out to them. 'Ahoy there! I'm a deputy marshal out of Billings. I reckon your captain's paroled to Jesus, but these murdering road agents are all accounted for. See if you can do anything for the girl while I get down off of this God damned roof.'

Martin was quick to respond. He detailed a number of men to head off down the riverbank equipped with ropes and staves, before leading others towards the steps up to the pilothouse. In all of this activity, no one noticed the furtive figure of Nelson Pruitt. That individual had carefully made his way over to the landing area and was now sizing up the state of affairs from behind the second wagon. He swiftly decided that all was not lost. If the marshal could be taken unawares and gunned down like the dog that he was, then he, Pruitt, could easily contain the situation until the victorious Dutch Henry re-joined him.

As Bronson walked back across the deckhouse roof, he was completely oblivious to the developing threat. Bairstow's continued absence was puzzling him to be sure, but he saw no reason not to put down his shotgun, so as to aid his descent on to the log pile. It was as he sat with his legs dangling over the edge that he suddenly realized his awful vulnerability, but by then it was too late!

For the second time that day, Dutch Henry's probing fingers closed around Samuel Bairstow's neck. As the terrible choking pressure increased, the Mountie desperately summoned an explosive burst of power. Left and right combination punches slammed into the giant outlaw's midriff and for a brief moment his vice-like grip loosened. The lawman wrenched free, but instead of backing rapidly out of reach he did the exact opposite. Ducking around under the outstretched arms, he viciously jabbed his boot into the back of Dutch Henry's right knee. With a cry of pain that man fell forward on to both his knees. Bairstow seized the moment and locked his powerful right arm around his opponent's throat. He dearly wished to reach for either his knife or revolver, so as to finish it there and then, but it was not to be.

Up against such a powerful adversary, the Canadian had no choice other than to use his left arm as a lock to increase the pressure. The alternative was to be shaken off like a rag doll. Gritting his teeth, he clung on in sheer desperation. Little by little the veins in Dutch Henry's neck began to bulge and his face grew florid. It seemed as though the frenzied death grip was gradually taking effect. Then, almost unbelievably, Bairstow felt himself being lifted clean off the floor.

With an almost inhuman grunt, his bear-like enemy got back on his feet, but even Dutch Henry realized that if he couldn't break the stranglehold he would soon return to his knees for good. Summoning his last reserves of strength, he abruptly launched himself back towards the stable wall. With a tremendous splintering crash, the two of them slammed into the timber. Bairstow took the brunt of the collision and as the air was forced from his lungs, so too did his death grip fall away.

With a shuddering gasp, the massive outlaw staggered free, completely unhindered by his opponent. The Canadian was just too winded to pursue. He lay against the splintered wood, desperately trying to get his breath. The two men had effectively fought themselves to a standstill, but it was Dutch Henry who first came to terms with that unsettling reality. Never before in his adult life had he been bested in a fight, possibly because he had never come up against so determined an opponent. It was that thought which prompted his decision to finally resort to firearms. And it was here that he held the advantage. His revolver was merely tucked in his belt, whereas the Mountie's Adams was securely held in a flap holster in the military fashion.

By a strange chance, it was at that moment that their eyes locked together. Both favoured the other with a dark brooding glance and in an almost supernatural moment of perception, Bairstow suddenly realized just what was to follow. Employing the strength of sheer desperation, he used the wall for leverage and hurled himself across the loft space. Frantically the other man reached for his Colt, but he was still dazed and slow to react. Just as his finger curled round the trigger, the lawman's full weight slammed into him.

Dutch Henry no longer possessed the wherewithal to withstand such a blow. Together the two men careered uncontrollably back to the edge of the floor boarding and into the void beyond. The sickening thud, as they struck the compressed earth floor, combined with the muffled roar of a powerful handgun. Both men lay unmoving, but the horses in the stalls around them stirred restlessly as they smelt the unmistakeable odour of charred flesh.

The ghastly shock of being completely immersed in freezing water quite literally took Kirsty's breath away. Her head and shoulders had hit first and she was terrifyingly aware that the river seemed to be drawing her deeper. The heavy winter clothing encasing her body was sodden and made all movement difficult. It was only the young woman's burning desire to survive that generated the terrific energy required to pump her way back up.

She broke the surface gasping for breath and was immediately overwhelmed by the powerful current. As she swept past the *Ethan Allen*'s stern, a voice bellowed out something unintelligible and there was a loud splash close by. Twisting her head, Kirsty spotted a big section of timber paralleling her course down the mighty river. It was her only chance of survival and she knew it.

Fighting against the dead weight of her saturated overcoat, she desperately paddled towards the diminutive raft. Those few feet seemed to require an inordinate amount of effort from her numbed limbs, but finally she made it. Seizing hold of the gnarled wood, she heaved with all her strength and gradually managed to get her upper body out of the icy water. With her teeth chattering and her lips turning blue, Kirsty frantically scrutinized the terrain ahead. Fate was kind, because she immediately observed just what she needed. Off to her right, stretching as far as the eye could see, the riverbank had eroded so that it was almost level with the fast-flowing river. That was her chance!

Willing her frozen legs into action, she kicked out towards the bank with a renewed energy that only a youngster could possess. Almost imperceptibly, the makeshift raft began to veer off to the right. Her breath came in ragged bursts as she struggled not to swallow the bitingly cold liquid. And then, unbelievably, her right boot struck solid ground. Suddenly Kirsty was no longer swimming, but pushing against the uneven riverbed.

It was whilst thrusting the suddenly heavy wood on to gravel that her strength finally gave out. With a shuddering sigh, the half-drowned young woman collapsed on to the timber. The water still lapped around her legs and her fine features were completely ashen. It was in this comatose state that the crew of the *Ethan Allen* found her a short time later.

With a satisfying snarl of triumph, Nelson Pruitt arose from behind the wagon and aimed his Winchester at the tin shield on Bronson's chest. The lawman had just dropped on to the woodpile and was minus his shotgun.

'You kilt my brother, you butcher!'

The marshal grabbed the side of the building with his only hand and peered over at the red-faced outlaw. His whiskery features betrayed no hint of the alarm that he had to be feeling and his reply was surprisingly mild. 'I gave Taylor the chance to surrender, same as you. Why don't you learn something from what happened at Fallowfield's Store and hand them guns over?'

The other man stared at him in total bewilderment. One twitch of his finger and the law dog was dead. Yet there he was, large as life, telling him to surrender. It really did beat all! A burning rage flared up inside him that effectively blocked out all logical thought, which of course was exactly what Bronson desired. In a strangely high-pitched tone, Pruitt screamed out, 'Get down on your knees, you poxed cur! I'll have you begging for your life before this day is out.'

Bronson snorted derisively. 'You'll have to give me some time on that. As you can see, I'm a mite beaten up.'

That was all too much for the incandescent outlaw. With his sweaty finger tightening on the trigger, he howled out, 'You God damned law d—'

The high-powered bullet came from behind and struck him in his right shoulder. It quite literally spun him around, so that he was no longer facing the hated lawman. Remarkably, his own rifle was still unfired and so it was an injured, but still dangerous Nelson Pruitt who stared in total bewilderment at his assailant. 'You! I thought you was dead.'

'Not hardly,' came the weary response.

With blood gushing from his agonizing wound, Pruitt finally lost all sense of reality and raised the muzzle of his Winchester.

'Again!' bellowed Bronson.

Sure enough, the weapon discharged a second time. On this occasion the bullet slammed into the outlaw's throat and there could no longer be any doubt about his most definite demise. In a welter of blood, Nelson Pruitt irrevocably joined his brother in the hereafter.

For a few moments, the only sounds that could be heard were of the distressed horses still tethered to the crippled wagon. It was Jesse Bronson who spoke first. 'Never took you for a back-shooter, Samuel!'

That man signed gently before favouring him with a lopsided smile, although in truth the greeting was hard to discern. The Mountie was quite literally drenched with blood, whilst his face appeared to have been pulverized in a meat market. The sticky liquid coating his torso appeared to be his, whereas that on his breeches obviously belonged to someone else. It was only with difficulty that he spoke. 'So that's both brothers accounted for, eh? I dare say you'll be going after their sisters and aunts and such next!'

It was the marshal's turn to smile, as he gestured towards the first wagon. 'No, but you'd better get yourself cleaned up. It's going to take some work shifting all those crates and

I've only got the one arm!'

Bairstow's response was drowned out by an angry yell from Jacques Labeau. 'I'm bleeding to death over here, you bastards!' That man was still manacled to the stern-wheeler. The Metis's continued survival abruptly reminded the Mountie that their attractive companion was nowhere to be seen. 'Where the hell's Kirsty got to?' he anxiously demanded through mashed lips.

Bronson's expression turned dark as he reached up for his sawn-off. 'You'd best ask Labeau about that.'

Confusion registered on the other man's features, but he had no time to form a question. From further down the riverbank there came a loud yell. A group of crewmen were carrying what looked like a body wrapped in a thick blanket. The two men reacted in markedly different ways. With a horrified expression on his features, Bairstow staggered off towards them, whilst Bronson dropped down to the deck and moved off towards his shackled prisoner. That individual regarded the grim-faced lawman with great unease. Labeau was visibly weakened by his leg wound and suddenly greatly regretted attracting the marshal's attention.

Bronson stopped directly before the half-breed and jabbed the shotgun's muzzles hard under his chin. His words contained a pent up anger that chilled the Metis to his core. 'I'm a federal officer, sworn to uphold the law, but you can believe one thing for certain. If that young girl is dead, I will take this badge off and then squeeze both triggers, so help me God!'

CHAPTER FIFTEEN

'Why are you tending to that animal? I want to see him hang this very hour, do you hear?' demanded Kirsty shrilly. 'It's only right and proper. That bastard murdered my pa and tried to kill me too.'

The three former voyageurs were huddled in the town jail. The citizens of Great Falls had built it in expectation of recruiting a sheriff, but so far no one had volunteered for the position. Jacques Labeau lay prostrate in the only cell, as the local sawbones worked to extract the bullet from his leg. His cries of anguish were loud and frequent, possibly because nobody had felt inclined to offer him any laudanum. The young woman, swaddled in a heavy blanket given to her by a crewman from the *Ethan Allen*, was gazing bleakly through the bars of the cell. She was still weak from her ordeal, but had insisted on confronting her father's killer.

Bronson shook his head regretfully. 'That may well happen, but not here and not now. My instructions are to take this scumsucking low-life back to Billings. After that he's out of my hands, but' – he glanced over at a battered, but clearly embarrassed Bairstow – 'Labeau may well get a noose up in Canada for crimes committed there, unless of course the God damned British Empire still goes in for flogging.'

Despite feeling desperately tired and vulnerable, Kirsty was beginning to get good and angry as well. She glared over at the unfortunate Mountie. 'He should hang for murder in Montana and you know it!'

Bairstow shrugged and favoured her with a genuine smile. 'Maybe he should and maybe he shouldn't, but I'm neither a judge nor a politician so it really isn't up to me.'

At that moment the doctor emitted a satisfied grunt and dropped a piece of bloody lead into a tin bowl. Simultaneously, his patient released a great howl and abruptly sat up. He was obviously in great pain, but also angry at his brutal treatment.

Moving clear of the two lawmen, Kirsty entered the cell and glared at him. Labeau's eyes met hers and even though in great distress a suggestive leer suddenly appeared on his pain-wracked features. 'Huh, you must be a lot tougher than your pa, as well as a whole heap prettier.'

Irrational rage surged through her like a lightning bolt and she moved forward to strike him. His left arm was manacled to the bunk, but of course that did not concern him over much. With snakelike speed, his right hand dropped to the hidden sheath in his boot. Even though in great discomfort, the Metis had goaded the young woman and then timed his strike to perfection.

Labeau's fingers slipped into the top of his scabbard, only for him to freeze rigid with surprise. Kirsty was both frightened and puzzled at his strange response to her approach, but then the marshal sidled up next to her and all became clear. In his hand, Bronson held a wicked looking skinning knife.

'I wondered when you'd miss this,' he remarked lightly. 'It must have slipped out of your boot when you briefly lost consciousness on the boat.'

As total silence settled over the jailhouse, the lawman reflectively balanced the knife on his palm, before turning to the young woman. 'Here, why don't you take it and finish the job?' he asked mildly.

As she recoiled slightly, Labeau cried out, 'Are you mad? I'm supposed to be your prisoner!'

Completely ignoring him, Bronson abruptly thrust the blade towards her and demanded, 'What's it to be, little lady, vengeance or the law?'

As the marshal knew so well, very few people could kill with a knife in cold blood. It was just too personal and immediate. And as expected, Kirsty shook her head in disgust and backed away.

'Very well,' he stated with obvious satisfaction. 'It looks like the law will just have to take its course, won't it?'

'You bastard,' wailed the Metis. 'You'd have let her carve me up for fun!'

'Oh, you'd better believed it, *monsieur*,' Bronson retorted sarcastically. 'But luckily for you, she's got scruples!'

It was five days later when the four heavily garbed riders set off on the one hundred and sixty mile trip to Billings. A lot had happened in the intervening time, including the digging of a great many graves. It had taken fully four men just to lift the blood-soaked corpse of Dutch Henry Bruckner out of the livery. He had finally come up against a man who couldn't be merely bludgeoned into submission. And then, just as the mass grave for the various outlaws had finally been filled in and the citizens had breathed a collective sigh of relief, the frozen body of Black Bart had been discovered on the hillside.

First Officer Martin was now the acting captain of the *Ethan Allen* and it was into his care that the crates from the second raft had been entrusted, along with those from the remaining wagon. Racine's damaged vehicle had been lifted back on to dry land by use of a block and tackle, but its cargo was lost until the summer, when a much lower and warmer river would hopefully allow for the recovery of the heavy crates.

As Great Falls disappeared into the distance, Marshal Bronson carefully scrutinized his three companions. Jacques Labeau was manacled to the saddle-horn and presented a sullen and dejected figure. His heavily bandaged leg had mended sufficiently to allow them to undertake the long journey, but it was obvious that he held little hope for his future prospects. The lawman's own arm was still in a loose sling, but did not trouble him greatly. It was as his glance fell on Kirsty Landers that he shook his head in puzzlement.

'For the life of me, young lady, I can't understand why you've insisted on making this trip,' he announced. 'You could have travelled on the *Ethan Allen* in some comfort and overseen the sale of that ore.'

In some ways, Bronson was the most perceptive of men and yet he was totally blind to what had passed between the two younger people. Bairstow's eyes met Kirsty's and he shook his head in amusement. It was left to her to explain the situation and so she reined in next to the marshal. Gesturing towards the gloomy prisoner, she stated, 'I mean to see that son of a bitch brought to justice, come what may. If that means travelling on to Canada with the corporal, then so be it. There is nothing left for me in Alder Gulch and I think I may just have found a new friend, if you take my meaning.'

Deputy US Marshal Jesse Bronson glanced from one to the other in bewildered surprise. Oh, he took her meaning all right. Spitting a stream of tobacco on to the iron hard ground, he remarked, 'Well, I'll be damned!'